Novels by Jessica Tilles

Anything Goes

In My Sisters' Corner

Apple Tree

Sweet Revenge

Fatal Desire

Erogenous Zone: A Sexual Voyage
Editor and Contributing Author
August 2007

"I dwell in possibility."
– Emily Dickinson

Acknowledgements

Writing a novel is easier for me, than writing the acknowledgments. The last thing I would want to do is exclude someone. So, if I leave anyone out, please blame it on the early stages of Alzheimer's, and not my heart.

Thank you. . .

Heavenly Father for blessing me with the creativity, talent, and gift of writing, and the passion for literature. Because of You, I am able to write, publish and care for my parents full-time. God is good, all of the time.

Mom and Dad, Jesse and Wallace Wright, for being the best parents a child could ever ask for. It means the world to me to be able to take care of you, as you did me, for the last forty years. I love you both!

Herbert Lipscomb, my big brother, for always being so supportive of my work and telling everyone about your little sister and her books.

Leslie Walker…you started this journey with me five years ago. You helped me take flight and, once my wings were strong enough for me to fly on my own, you stood back in the shadows and watched me soar. Thanks, Diva!

To my sisters, Valerie Wright, Sheila Wright, Colleen Green, and Jacqueline Johnson, for being my inspiration to pen *In My Sisters' Corner*.

Cassius Titus, Esquire, for being great legal counsel for Xpress Yourself Publishing and always being there when I need you. I owe you, BIG TIME!

Gary A. Johnson, publisher of Black Men In America.com and author of *25 Things that Really Matter in Life*. I have said this numerous times, and I will continue to say it. Your picture should be in Webster's next to the word *friend* because you, more than anyone I know, are the epitome of friend. So many times, you covered me, when you really did not have to. Thank you for showing me true characteristics of friendship.

Darlene Stukes, my muse, for being the inspiration that became my most memorable character. Raven is a pistol, and so are you! I would not have you any other way, Joe. Little do people know that Raven is alive and well, walking the streets of the DC Metropolitan Area, as frisky as she wants to be! Skank you, Cuz!

Xpress Yourself Publishing family: Bill Holmes, author of *One Love* and *Straight From My Heart*, Makenzi, author of *Dangerously* and *That's How I Like It*, Nyah Storm, *Confessions of Sex Therapist*, Kenda Bell, author of *For Every Love There Is A Reason*, Michael J. Burt, author of *Love Changes*, Lonnie Spry, author of *How Do I Go On?*, Mia A. Moore, author of *Tonight I Give In*, Gayle Jackson Sloan, author of *Saturday's Child, Wednesday's Woes,* and *Let the Necessary Occur*, Sherman Barrett, author of *How Men Cheat*, Elissa Gabrielle, author of *Good to the Last Drop* and *A Whisper to a Scream*, Nataki Suggs, author of *A Life Beyond Limits: Overcoming Private Pain*, Sumumba Sobukwe, author of *Dating Game: A Brother Speaks Up,*

Tinisha Nicole Johnson, author of *Searchable Whereabouts*. Y'all keep me on my toes! It is with great pleasure that I take part in making your dreams, as published authors, come true. You have made my dreams come true too. I am so proud of all of you. We are family!

William Fredrick Cooper, author of *Six Days in January* and *There's Always A Reason*. My friend, 2007 is your year. Do me a favor…open your heart and welcome all blessings, which *will* flow, as you would not believe! Remain positive and know that no weapon formed against you will prosper.

To all of the wonderful book clubs, especially the Jackson Mississippi Readers Club and Turning Pages Book Club, who have supported, and continue to support, me throughout the years.

To the staff at Karibu Books for your continued support of the Xpress Yourself Publishing family. Your support and generosity does not go unnoticed or unappreciated.

To all of my kin folks in Emporia, Virginia; Orlando, Florida; Chicago, Illinois; Southampton, New York; New York City; California; Washington, DC; Maryland; Dallas, Texas; Philadelphia, Pennsylvania; Thornburg, Virginia; and Courtland, Virginia for all of your love and support!

Ricardo Warfield, I wait with bated breath. So far, so good.

If I left anyone out, write your name here _____.

If you keep reading, I'll keep writing!

Jessica Tilles
Sunday, April 1, 2007
2:56 a.m.

UNFINISHED BUSINESS

Jessica Tilles

Chapter 1

As the black Mercedes-Benz SL 500 idled in the driveway, slender, French-manicured fingers tapped the steering wheel, rhythmically to 50 Cent's *In The Club*. Morgan's head bounced, as she mouthed the hip-hop lyrics. Gazing at the five-thousand-square-foot home Arthur surprised her with after their brief separation two years ago. "A new house for a new beginning," he had told her when he escorted her through the massive maple oak double doors. *A new beginning my ass,* she thought. *Humph!*

She loved everything about the house; it wouldn't be long before she would hear the pitter-patter of Franklin's tiny feet scampering across the black and white linoleum foyer. She couldn't imagine living anywhere else, this was home.

Living with Arthur, after his transgression, however, was another story. Morgan wasn't strong enough, nor could she find it in her heart, to forgive him, despite how hard he was trying to make things right. Franklin needed his father on a full-time basis. She knew how deprived she felt not having paternal guidance in her life, and she refused to have her son experience the same hurtful emotions. However, it was going to be hard.

With a resigned sigh, Morgan leaned her head back against the headrest. Whipping Raven's ass took a toll on her, leaving her physically, mentally and emotionally exhausted. Her heart now broken, she never wanted to speak to her sister again. Repeated images of Arthur and Raven intertwined haunted her.

"Oh, Mama, what am I going to do?" She spoke in a soft, serene voice, as a crystal drop graced her cheek. "I wish you were here. I so need your guidance?" Wiping it away, she lowered her head as she continued reflecting on this condition. "A demon seed," she whispered, repeating the words her father once spoke to her in a dream. "You were right, Daddy."

As she slowly raised her head, Morgan's eyes opened to Arthur standing in the front door, smiling and waving at her.

Hissing at him in resentment, while rolling her eyes, she snapped her head to the left. The sight of him nauseated her. Torn between conflicting emotions; part of her felt awful. Yet at the same time, she wanted to be so mean to him, blatantly belligerent, hell bent on making him pay for his indulgence with her sister. She felt he deserved every bit of her anger as well.

Detecting, and then decoding her internal war, Arthur's smile turned upside down, as he stepped back inside the house and closed the door.

Grabbing her purse, Morgan proceeded to exit the car, but the ringing of her cell phone stopped her. She pulled the cell from her purse, looked at the caller ID, and rolled her eyes upward once more. "What is it?" she barked into the tiny hand-held instrument.

Arthur frowned up his face and stuck out his bottom lip. He knew what he did was wrong, but how long was she going to hold it against him? He was trying so hard to do everything right to make up for his fuck up. "Honey, are you all right?"

"I'm fine. Why are you wasting my minutes?" she snapped, spewing venom directly at his heart.

Arthur was quiet for a moment. For fear the evil monster he undoubtedly created would bite his head off, he was afraid to say another word. Treading to the center of her frigid lake, he was walking on thin ice and knew if he weren't careful, he would fall through.

"Fucking idiot," she mumbled beneath her breath, but loud enough for him to hear.

Bravely, he cleared his throat and proceeded to speak, his voice barely above a whisper. "I have a hot bubble bath waiting for you, honey."

"Did I ask you to run me a goddamn bath?"

Arthur gasped, but remained silent. Some how he understood how Kane, from *Menace II Society*, felt when the cops eloquently stated, "Now you see, you know you fucked up, right?"

As his mind played games on him, Morgan felt awful. Relaxing her shoulders and sighing heavily, "Thank you," she said, a smile creeping at the corner of her mouth. "That was nice of you."

"Morgan, I do love you. I know I can't right the wrong I've committed, and I wouldn't blame you if you decided to leave me–"

"I'm not leaving my house," she snapped her voice sharp and filled with smugness. "If you want to leave, then get the fuck out. However, I'm not going anywhere. Do you hear me?"

Arthur didn't want to get into another blow up, for he knew the result would not be a positive one. "I'm not leaving either." His voice trembled, as he tried to soothe things over. "Your bath is getting cold."

"Drain the tub," she coldly ordered. He had pissed her off and she didn't feel like being a loving wife toward a man who had defiled her bed and committed the ultimate betrayal. Before disconnecting the call, Morgan shouted, "Fuck you," and tossed the phone onto the passenger seat. Leaning her head against the steering wheel, she tried to cry away her heartache, but the harder she cried, the more her head hurt, and the angrier she became.

Morgan took her time entering the house. Coming face to face with Arthur wasn't something she was looking forward to encountering; she couldn't bear it. Closing the door behind her, she dropped her purse to the floor, kicked off her shoes, leaned back against the door, dejected, and defeated. Aside from bloodshot eyes from a thirty-minute crying festival, her head was pounding and she craved peace and quiet. She hoped Franklin was down and napping, quietly.

Arthur sat on the bottom step, his head hung low as he glared at the floor.

"Where's Franklin?" Her voice was solemn.

"He's taking a nap."

"Did you give him his bath?"

Avoiding eye contact, Arthur nodded his head, clasped his hands together and twiddled his thumbs. "What happened with Raven?"

"She got off easy," she said, her iceberg disposition returned, rolling her eyes and turning her head to the side. "I wish I had a cigarette."

"You don't smoke," he chuckled softly, hoping to break the tension.

Sliding her back down the door, she sat on the floor and stretched her legs out before.

The pause, though only for second, seemed like hours to Arthur. The guilt he felt was playing mind games. Finally ending the impasse, he shrugged his shoulders. "I fucked up, Mo."

"Yes you did and in a big way too." Morgan tossed her keys on the floor and watched them slide across the bare floor. "I never cheated on you, Arthur. Humph, I never even thought about it. I suppose," she continued sarcastically. "I wouldn't know how to cheat." Then, she glared into his remorseful eyes in an attempt to pierce his heart the way he knifed hers. "But if I find me someone to fuck, preferably *your* brother, that would make it even. No?"

Sighing heavily, Arthur prepared himself; once again, for the tongue-lashing he knew she was famous for inducing. Morgan's words cut deeper than any punishment she could bestow upon him.

He brushed his hands through his curly tresses, down to the back of his neck where he threaded his fingers together. He needed a haircut. Unable to stop fidgeting, he ran his hand across his five o'clock shadow. He needed a shave too.

"Even when we were separated, I never cheated on you. Don't get me wrong, the temptation was there, but I loved you more than anything."

"You're using past tense. You don't love me anymore?"

"Yes, I still love you. I can't stand your ass at the moment, but I can't stop loving someone at the drop of a hat either."

Exhaling discreetly, Arthur felt a sense of relief. She still loved him. He smiled inside.

Morgan looked down at the floor and then at her toes. She wiggled them, flexed her foot and then pointed her toes toward him. "Not even my sister. Regardless of how she betrayed me, I still love her. I knew Raven was capable of many things, but her fucking you…well, I guess it really shouldn't surprise me in the least." She gently tapped her head against the door. "There was nothing I wouldn't do for Raven. Her back was always secure as long as I was around. It would've been nice to know what it felt like for my sister to have had my back, every once in a while. Humph, all the shit I got that girl out of."

"She's sick. She has a problem." Immediately after the comment left his mouth, Arthur wished he could press rewind. *Damn!*

Morgan gave him another menacing look into his eyes and hesitated. "What's your excuse?"

Arthur noticed the warmth was no longer there; and it terrified him. "My actions were inexcusable and I'm beating myself up for it. We've overcome so many obstacles and I know we can overcome this." Falling on his knees and crawling toward her, "Please don't give up on me, Morgan," he begged. Reaching her toes, he leaned down and kissed each toe. "I don't want to think of living life without you."

She tilted her head to the side and gnawed on her bottom lip. "Did you kiss her toes? You've never kissed my toes before now."

Damn, Arthur thought, as he dropped his weight on her legs in defeat. "How long are you going to make me pay?"

"Forever!"

His warrior's pride shattered, Arthur buried his face between her calve muscles and sobbed. "Oh God, Morgan."

Seeing her man's broken spirit, Morgan's face softened. She pouted her lips and reached for his head, running her fingers through his hair and down to his cheek, pulling him up toward her. Staring deep into his eyes, she noticed that the sparkle was gone from his pupils.

They were gone from hers as well, for she no longer trusted him.

He pulled himself closer to her face and grazed her lips with his. "I'll do what ever it takes," he whispered, his tongue stroking her bottom lip.

Her lips trembled as she softly moaned his name, giving him more hope.

Arthur's eyes remained opened, peering through to her soul, hopeful while hurting, trying to find an ounce of forgiveness. Not expecting to be pardoned really, he knew the journey to righting this ship was going to be a hard road to travel. However, he was willing to endure it no matter how bumpy or how far. Until death do us part, was his vow and he was sticking to it. Was she?

He slid his hand up her thigh, to her abdomen, finding comfort caressing her breast.

Morgan inhaled quickly, while drawing her eyes tighter, squeezed out a single tear, causing a thin stream to flow down her cheek. She shook her head defiantly.

"Not now, baby. Not now, don't turn me away," Arthur encouraged.

His tongue savored the saltiness of her skin as his lips brushed her ear, traveling across her cheek, down her lips, and then tasting the sweetness of her mocha cream-flavored lip-gloss.

Morgan's lips trembled against his. "You need a condom," she whispered.

The unaccustomed request sent chills throughout Arthur. Stopping, he pulled himself up on his knees and squared his shoulders. "I need a what?"

"You've been with someone else. I need to protect myself."

"Protect yourself from what?"

"Arthur, you had sex with another woman."

"For God's sake, Morgan, I can't keep doing this."

"Then do what you have to do."

"What's that supposed to mean?"

Morgan shrugged her shoulders. "However you perceive it. Shit, Shalimar said it best, 'make that move, right now, baby.'" She snatched up her shoes and headed toward the stairs. "I don't want you in the bed anymore. Since you're not leaving the house, then you should move your things into the guest room."

"Aww come on, Morgan. Now you're being ridiculous," Arthur shouted angrily as saliva sprayed from his mouth.

"I suggest you use Hannah and her five sisters," his wife announced sarcastically, pointing in the direction of her punany. "Or better yet, get some ass from Raven, because you're never going to touch this ass again!" Her message emphatically delivered, she stormed up the stairs, into the bedroom and slammed the door.

Arthur slouched against the wall. Peering downward at his crotch, his dick was hard as a two-by-four.

"I'm not giving up, Morgan," he yelled up the stairs to a closed door.

Inside his home office, Arthur moved behind his massive oak desk and retrieved the tube of Vaseline petroleum jelly from the side draw. He unscrewed the cap, squeezed a large amount into the palm of his hand and tossed the tube back into the draw, before unzipping his pants. Pulling back the opening of his boxers and allowing his flaccidity to breathe, he leaned his back against the high back chair and wrapped his greased hand around his penis. Closing his eyes, he pictured Morgan naked and stroked vigorously, wishing the lubrication was, instead, the warmth and wetness of her love. Speeding up the tempo, slowing it down, then renewing his excitement again, as the friction heightened, his lips parted and silent moans escaped from his mouth.

Suddenly, his thoughts of Morgan transformed to shared moments with Raven. Stroking harder and harder, getting more excited at the arousal created from his self-manipulated sex, Arthur moaned and groaned as he pushed the chair back away from the desk. Closing in on his nirvana by masturbation, he stretched his legs out before him as the creamy white thickness oozed from the opening, over his fingers and down his shaft. He looked down at the mess in total disgust.

"This is fucking ridiculous!"

Chapter 2

"I can't believe I'm doing this," she mumbled to herself. "I can't believe I have got my tail out here like this."

Jo pulled into the driveway, parked her car and stared blankly in front of her. She inhaled deeply, turned off the engine and took one last look in the rearview mirror.

"This is absolutely ridiculous," she bitched. "He is going to think I have lost my mind."

She slid out the car and reached in the back for her bag of tricks. She closed the car door, placed her bag on the roof of the car and adjusted her attire. Grabbing the bag, she headed toward the front door. It was too late for her to turn back. She pressed her index finger against the doorbell and waited impatiently.

The turn of the locks made her legs shake. She'd never done anything like this before and she wasn't quite sure what to do. She'd seen it on HBO's *Real Sex* and figured she'd give it a try. As the door opened, her body stiffened like a board, no flexibility, whatsoever.

The smile across her face was forced and her bottom lip trembled. She was scared out of her mind. What would he think of her?

As the door opened, Jo yelled, "Surprise!"

Chas stood before her with his mouth wide opened. Jo was a remarkable sight and the front of his pants was growing tighter.

Her forced smile turned into a frown. "I look like a whore."

"Woman, you look stunning."

She perked up. "Really…"

"Yes!" Chas stepped back for her to enter. "Get in here before the world sees all of what you have to offer," he chuckled.

The black, full-length, sheer negligee, with black and blue matching bra and panty, accentuated every curve of her round hips and apple bottom booty. The stiletto heels exposed the musculature of her thighs.

Damn, baby got some serious ass, he thought sizing her up from head the toe and from one hip to the next, enjoying the view from where he stood.

"Don't move. I'll be right back!" Jo darted up the stairs and into the bedroom, closing the door behind her. She emptied the contents from her bag and looked around the room. She placed a candle on each available spot. She reached into her purse and pulled out her favorite Alfred Sung scent, *Shi*, and sprayed it in the air. She grabbed the book of matches, struck one and lit the candles. She walked over to the CD player and searched for something romantic. She'd forgotten to bring her music, so whatever Chas had would have to do. She eyed a seventies slow jam CD and slid it into the player. She pressed play and waited to hear the first selection. Heatwave crooned *Always and Forever*, followed by The O'Jay's and *Stairway to Heaven*.

"Perfect," she smiled, taking one last glimpse into the mirror. She slid her hands over her curvaceous hips, propped up her breast and pursed her lips together. Opening the door, she beckoned for Chas. When she heard his footsteps ascending the stairs, she darted for the bed and seductively positioned herself across the king-sized featherbed, her legs crossed and lips pouted—an African American version of Marilyn Monroe's seductive pin-up.

Chas slowly opened the door and stood before her. "What is all of this?"

"It's all for you."

"Woman, you are something else."

"Come a little closer, sweetie. Don't be scurred," she chuckled.

Chas belted out a hearty laugh. "Not to worry. You don't scare me."

"So what are you waiting for?"

Folding his arms across his chest, "Contemplating my next move," he smirked.

He untied the string around his waist and slipped out of the fleece sweat pants. Pulling his shirt over his head, exposing his bulging biceps and protruding nipples, he aimed directly at her, craving to be inside her where he would wallow in her sweetness. He approached the bed and placed his hands on her knees, and stroked her legs down to her ankles and then lifting the long, black sheer sheath up her legs, over her thighs and back to her waist. He spread her thighs apart, leaned in toward her love and inhaled deeply.

Jo placed her index finger between her supple lips and gently bit down. She felt her juices soaking through the crotch of her panty. She raised her leg and rested it on his shoulder, as she wrapped the other leg around his waist, pulling him closer. She raised her hips and stroked her crotch against his abdomen. She cooed, enjoying the sensations of having something rubbing against her clitoris.

Suddenly, Chas pulled back from her.

Jo raised her head. "What's wrong? Why did you stop?"

"Let's play a game."

"Play a what?"

"A game, I want to play a game."

Annoyed, Jo plopped her head on the bed and lowered her legs. "What kind of game?"

Chas reached into the drawer of his nightstand and retrieved two white dice. He rattled them in his closed hand.

Jo was getting more annoyed and out of the mood. "You want to play dice?"

"Yeah, but these are different."

"Baby, I don't want to play anybody's dice," she whined. "I want to spend quality time with my sweetie."

"You are spending quality time with me and you'll love this game." He reached his hand out toward her. "Come on, get up. Let's play!"

They sat a leg length from each other on the bed as he tossed the dice onto the bed.

"Lick. Toes," she chuckled. "Is this what you passed up the good stuff for?"

"Don't worry, I'll get to the good stuff soon enough. Now, you have to lick my toes."

Jo laughed hysterically. "You want me to what?" She couldn't stop laughing. She'd seen Chas' feet and they definitely weren't toes she wanted to lick. "Boy, you'll need ten pedicures before I put my lips to your feet!" She held tight to her abdomen. "You better roll again, brother man."

Chas tried to look as though his feelings were hurt, but the smile on his face couldn't be suppressed. "I've seen your feet too, for the record."

Jo's laughter disappeared. "What are you trying to say about my feet? I have pretty feet, thank you very much."

"Yes, well, all mothers think new born babies are cute too."

Jo reached around and popped Chas upside the head. "Just roll the damn dice."

He tossed the dice toward her. "It's your turn and I won't back out either."

Jo shrugged and rolled the dice. "Lick. Question mark. What does that mean?"

"The question mark is anything you want. Umm, if you want me to lick *your* toes or lick your body…anything you want licked."

Jo curled up the corner of her lips, throwing him a seductive look. Now she could get down to the business at hand and toss those dice back where they belonged, in the drawer. She leaned back on the bed, rising up on her elbows. Propping the heels of her feet on the edge of the bed, she spread her legs. "Lick my clit."

"For how long?"

"What do you mean?"

"It has to be either thirty or sixty seconds."

"Shit, lick it until I say stop."

"Nope, it has to be thirty or sixty seconds."

Jo rolled her eyes and pouted. "I don't like this game."

Chas shook his head and chuckled. "It sucks when you can't have your way, doesn't it?

She dropped in defeat. "Okay, I'll take sixty seconds."

Chas crawled between her opened legs and pushed the crotch of her panty to the side. "Whoowee, baby, you sure are wet down here."

Jo nudged him with her knee.

Chas leaned in, stuck out his tongue and stroked her protruding clitoris.

Her body heaved as she moaned with pleasure.

Keeping time, thirty seconds into the game, he used his index finger to lift the hood over her clitoris. He stroked his tongue around the clitoris, settling under the hood, where he focused for the remaining sixty seconds.

"I'm about to cum," she moaned. Her voice was deep, almost demonic. "Don't stop, baby."

Chas stopped.

Jo sprung upward. "I can't believe you did that!"

"Roll the dice," he playfully ordered.

Jo was reluctant and ready to call it quits. She was hot, horny and pissed off. He stopped as she was nearing the ultimate climax. She had never experienced this form of foreplay. She was frustrated as hell and ready to leave. She came over there, half-naked; to seduce him, not play games.

"It's your turn," she huffed.

"Aww baby, come on. Don't be that way." Chas leaned into her and softly caressed her neck with his lips. "Come on, baby. Don't be mad at me." He moved his lips to her ear and gently blew inside.

Jo continued pouting, trying to stay mad at him, but he was making it very difficult and she loved that about him. He knew exactly what to do. Chills shot throughout her body.

Stroking her inner thigh, Chas moved toward the welcoming warmth of her love.

Sighing seductively, Jo slowly dropped her head back and reclined to the bed. "Stop teasing me, babe," she cooed. "I feel like I'm about to explode."

Inching his long fingers along her sex, while masterly massaging her clitoris, "Ooh, you're soaked," he whispered, teasing her vaginal lips. Removing his finger, he tasted his woman. "Woman, I've never tasted anything so delicious in all my life." His words stimulated her more than his touch.

Heaving her body, Jo pulled down on his neck. "I want to feel you inside me."

Ignoring the hardness of his hooked heated steel, Chas smiled and continued with his mental foreplay. "You're not ready for me yet."

"I am! Please, I'm ready baby."

"Hmm, let me check it out," he said, removing her underwear. "You are dripping wet." He amused himself as he pleased her. Although he was hard as the Rock of Gibraltar and badly wanted to be inside her, stimulating her was more satisfying than an ejaculation.

Chas leaned into her sex and inhaled. Jo maintained a level of cleanliness he adored. Once again, he lightly feathered her clitoris with his finger.

Her body heaved, her legs shaking and her pants quick and short. In an uncontrollable fit, she grabbed the pillow and tossed it to the floor. "Oh my God," she cried out, her arms stretched wide above her head, fists bald up.

He knew he had her. Anytime a woman called out for God, she was ready to blow. Besides, her clitoris had swelled to the point where it was no longer covered by the hood, something he'd never seen before until he met her. He thought it to be quite fascinating how her clitoris would swell to the size of a tiny penis.

It was time and she was ready, as he wrapped his lips around her swollen bud. As he vigorously sucked, white cream expelled from her, dripping down his chin.

Chas stood to his feet and walked to closet, where he reached up and pulled a shoebox from the top shelf.

Unable to speak, with a spinning head, Jo watched him.

Chas returned before her with the box in hand. "How are you feeling?"

Shaking her head, she looked up at him and smiled, still unable to utter a single word.

"I'm not done with you yet." He opened the box and revealed two silver bullets attached to one controller.

Her eyes grew and she mustered the ability to speak. "What are you going to do with those?"

"Rock your world."

Jo bashfully covered her eyes. "Well, I have no complaint with you rocking anything!" She propped her feet on the edge of the bed. "Do what you do, Daddy."

"Ahh, I love it when you call me Big Papa," he toyed.

"Yeah, okay, *Big Papa.*"

Kneeling before his Goddess, he placed one of the cold silver vibrators inside her and placed the other snuggly between her vaginal lips, resting comfortably on her sensitive clitoris.

"Ooh, they are cold. You could've warmed them first."

"Not to worry, my love, they will warm up in no time, and so will you." Chas had totally flipped the coin with complete control and loved it, and so did she. He switched the control to the lowest speed, advancing speed with each heave of her body.

Jo raised her legs straight up, and then wrapped them around his neck. When he increased the speed to the highest level, her legs flew straight up again and both silver bullets shot from her, hitting him square between the eyes.

Chas fell to the floor in laughter. "Wow, that was massive!" He watched his woman roll over and over, eventually crashing to the floor. "Are you alright?"

Jo's pants were like a dog, craving for water. "What... what...what are you...doing with those?"

"Something I picked up today from the Pleasure Chest in Georgetown. Remember, your man will *always* be one step ahead of you."

Jo pulled herself to the bed and rested her chin on the down comforter. "What do you mean?"

"Nothing, baby." He leaned down, kissed her forehead and headed toward the bathroom.

Jo followed on his heels. "No, it's not 'nothing.' I don't want us communicating like that. Now, tell me what you meant by that statement."

Inside the bathroom, he turned to her, grabbed her face, and pulled her close to him. "Don't start getting paranoid on me. I was only saying that I had plans to give you total pleasure today, just as you had for me." He kissed her on the lips. "Now, may I please use the bathroom?"

"With a hard-on?"

"It'll go down."

"Oh baby, you didn't get yours."

"Yes I did," he smiled, "now, leave me be, woman!"

"I wanna watch."

"What?" Chas laughed. "If you don't get out of here..." He playfully shoved her into the hallway. "I won't be long. I'll miss you though," he said, closing the door.

Chapter 3

She gasped for air, shot straight up in the bed, and looked around the room. She was soaked, as if she had experienced a serious case of night sweats. She grabbed tightly to the sheets and looked around. Her pulse raced, as heat ravished through her body.

John stirred from his slumber and looked up at her in a sleepy daze. "What's wrong, honey?"

"I don't know," she panted.

He pulled himself up on his elbow and stroked her arm. "You are soaked. Did you have a bad dream?"

Deborah hunched her shoulders and lowered her head. She shook her head, finding it unbearable to hold back the tears. "John, I don't know."

"You don't know what? What's going on with you?"

Covering her face with her hands, she sobbed uncontrollably.

John was now upright in the bed, cradling her in his arms.

She wiped the tears from her eyes and buried her face in his chest. Deep sobs racked her insides. She tore herself away with a choking sob. "I don't know where to begin."

"You have my full attention."

John always knew there was a hidden issue within Deborah. Her aggressiveness in bed was the biggest warning. At first, he enjoyed the roughness of their sexual encounters. However, now it had become a turn-off. The time she wrapped her fingers around his throat during sex, scared him, and it was one he would never forget. He'd made the decision to deal with the issue when she was ready to face it.

"May I have some water?"

"Sure, babe…" John pulled the covers back and stood to his feet. His nakedness made it hard for her to tell her story. He was beautiful and perfectly chiseled, with broad shoulders and a sexy swagger.

He darted to the bathroom and returned with a Dixie cup of water. It wasn't quite what she had in mind. She wished he had gone downstairs to the kitchen for the water. It would've given her time to gather her thoughts.

"Thank you," she smiled, taking the cup and sipping the water.

John stood before her. "What's going on?"

With her head lowered, she peeked up at him. "Could you get back under the covers or put some clothes on?"

He crawled under the covers, fluffed the pillows against the headboard and leaned back. This better be good. He didn't know how much more he was going to be able to tolerate.

"There's something about my past I never shared with you."

"No better time than the present."

"Don't interrupt me, John. It'll only make it harder for me to get it out."

John nodded and gave her his full attention.

She took a deep sigh, closed her eyes and blew air from between her pursed lips. "When I was six years old, I woke up to my father's hand between my legs."

John leaned forward. He couldn't believe his ears. He refused to speak. She had the floor.

"He would do this every night. My mother worked late nights. I guess she was too tired to fuck him when she got home at six in the morning, so he finger fucked me instead."

Shock and disbelief heated his face. Actually, he was getting pissed and wanted to find the bastard and whip his ass. Her father had sexually molested his woman. What kind of sick bastard would do that to his own daughter? He tried to maintain his cool.

Deborah cried profusely. "This is why I'm so aggressive in bed. I can't help it. When ever I'm making love to you, I think back to my father and something comes over me."

"Do I remind you of your father?"

"No, it's the act of it all."

"I've had problems with past relationships because of my being so aggressive during lovemaking. I don't know, it's like when we are making love, I think back to my father and I snap."

24

"Well, did you ever tell anyone?" John lowered his head into the span of his hand. "The sick motherfucker," he mumbled.

"I told my mother and she slapped me as hard as she could."

"She didn't believe you?"

"Oh she believed me alright. She said it was my fault, packed me up and sent me to live with my grandmother."

"Well good. At least you got out from under him."

Deborah fell back onto the bed and pulled the covers over her head. "I haven't spoken to my mother since."

"You should call the police and have that perverted bastard locked up."

"I can't."

"Yes you can."

"He's dead."

John pulled back the covers and pulled her into him. "Baby, you need counseling. You need to find a way to come to terms with this…this awful experience."

"All I need is you," she whimpered.

"Baby, I can't help you. I mean I can be here for you. But, I can't help you work through the trauma. You need a professional."

"Will you go with me to the counseling sessions? I don't want to do it alone."

"Yes, of course. If you want me there, I'm there."

John slid down beneath the covers and cradled Deborah in his arms. Kissing her forehead, he vowed to help her through this. She had to resolve this issue before he asked her to take on his last name. He desperately wanted to make love to her, but remnants of the last episode lingered in his mind.

Chapter 4

Dressed in a purple robe, Cassie was looking in the refrigerator as Jay stood in the kitchen's archway. She closed the refrigerator and looked at him. Whores are better than sluts are. Whores get paid and sluts don't," Cassie said, with a chuckle before ending her call. "I'll talk to you later. I'm having a drink with a friend." She looked toward Jay and blew him a kiss. "I'd hate to be rude," she said, before ending the call.

He walked over to, and she took the unopened pack of cigarettes from his outstretched hand. He stood there.

She handed him a drink. "Well, sit the fuck down before you make the place look poor."

"That's real cute," Jay said, resting his lips on the rim of the brandy snifter. He inhaled the vanilla aroma of the naVan, a new brand of Courvosier he stumbled across while hanging out at Jasper's with the fellas. "So, we still on for Friday?"

Cassie frowned and sat down beside Jay.

"What's the look for?"

"Don't spill that shit on my white sofa."

Jay looked at her and smirked. "You're no virgin. So, what's with all the white furniture any damn way?"

"Aw, go to hell, Jay! Just don't spill that shit on my furniture."

Jay leaned in to her. "Or what you gon' do?"

Cassie leaned back and swallowed hard. She took her eyes off Jay and stared at the wall. She wasn't stupid. She'd experienced his bastard-like ways one time too many.

"That's what I thought." Jay leaned back and crossed his leg over his knee. "Did you take care of things?"

She hesitated before speaking. "Not yet, but I will though."

Jay lowered his head and sat the glass down on the table. "I thought you were going to take care of that, Cass." He rubbed his hands together, annoyed.

"Well, I haven't had the chance to do it."

"You wanna tell me when you were going to get the chance."

"I was going to call her back."

"Call her back?" Jay stood to his feet and huffed. "Damn it, Cass. How is this shit going to work if you don't follow through on your fucking end?"

"Don't cuss at me, Jay, and I can handle my end. You make sure your end is straight."

"My end is straight. Let's make sure we have the plans together."

"Friday night…here. Right?"

Jay nodded. "What time?"

"Eight o'clock should be a good time."

"You're taking care of the other specifics?"

"Confirmed it today. We are straight and ready to give that bitch exactly what she deserves."

Cassie gazed at the floor in deep thought. Marcy consumed her thoughts constantly, and today was no different. Memories of Marcy's funeral haunted her. A knot formed in her throat each time she envisioned Marcy resting peacefully in her casket, surrounded by soft pink and delicate lace.

"Oh God, Cassie," she cried, as she wrapped her arms around her waist.

For a minute, Jay felt bad for Cassie and reached out to her. He quickly withdrew. He didn't have it in him to comfort or console anyone. It wasn't a practiced behavior and he surely wasn't going to start now. But then again, there is always a first time for everything.

Jay leaned in and stretched his arm around her back, his hand resting on her thigh. "I miss her too."

She placed her hand on his forearm and glared into his deep, dark eyes. "She didn't deserve to die."

Jay was confused. He wasn't sure if he was feeling compassion for Cassie or lust. "Hush. Let's not talk about it." He reached for her chin and turned her face toward him. John Legend crooned, "You got me up so high," as he leaned in and kissed her supple lips. She didn't pull back.

His hand rested on her knee. Her legs slightly opened, allowing him passage to a place he hadn't ventured in quite some time. He wondered if it still felt the same, soft and wet, and extra tight.

He broke their embrace and stood to his feet. "What are we doing?"

Her chest heaved and her breaths deep and hard as if she ran a ten-mile marathon. She licked her lips and swallowed hard. "I don't know."

He unbuttoned the cuffs on his shirt. "This ain't right," he said, growing more excited.

"I know," she said, unbuttoning her blouse.

"So, we shouldn't do this, right?" He pulled off his shirt and dropped it to the floor.

She raised her hips up from the sofa and pulled her pants down around her knees and said, "I don't know."

"Shit! This feels so fucking right though," he said, removing his belt and flinging it across the room.

"Well, it's not like we've never done it before." She unsnapped her bra, pulled it over her arms and flung it across the room, landing beside his belt.

He admired her breast. They were large and firm, like sweet honeydew melons. He stood before her. His erect penis pointed straight at her.

Cassie tossed one long leg over the arm of the sofa, as she extended the other across the plush white-carpeted floor, her glistening lips exposed.

He could see it all—her plump clitoris peeking between her sweet vaginal lips. The soft, pinkish insides of her pussy were moist.

Gazing between her thighs, he wrapped his hands around his tool and licked his lips in anticipation of the forthcoming expedition inside her cave.

"Are you sure this is what you want?" She slid her middle finger in and out of her mouth, before sliding up inside her.

Watching her made him hard as hell. He dropped down to his knees and watched as her finger eased in and out of her wetness.

She removed her finger and slid it between his lips.

He closed his eyes and moaned.

She curled her finger inside his mouth and moved his head southward. His lips made a smacking noise when she removed her finger.

"Taste me," she ordered.

He obliged her by sucking and pulling at her clitoris. He remembered exactly how she liked it, quickly bringing her to a mind-blowing climax. He aimed to please.

He stood up and stepped closer to her. His erect member waited patiently.

She leaned forward and opened her mouth.

He moved his hips forward and slid inside her mouth.

Her eyes closed tight, as the shaft vanished into and then slid out of, the tight circle of her lips. Each time the head hit the back of her throat she shuddered with pleasure. She pulled back to lie down on the sofa.

He lay on top of her, his head at her sweet pussy, while his penis danced in her face.

She threw her leg over the back of the sofa and wrapped the other leg around the back of his neck. She grabbed hold of his penis and tasted his pre-come.

His fingers moved to her labia and slipped inside her sweetly slick pussy.

He reached for his pants, pulled them to him; he reached inside the pocket and pulled out a Trojan. Using his teeth to open the package, he stood up and slowly rolled the condom over his hardness, down to the shaft, careful not to catch any of the curly hairs.

His condom-covered penis disappeared inside her. She met his strokes, thrusting up. His face distorted as he concentrated heavily on fucking her harder and faster, as her orgasm neared. He was quiet, but she was unnecessarily loud. This had begun to annoy him. He attempted to tune her out, yet her yelling made him fuck her harder.

"Yes…fuck me…fuck me…fuck me, you bastard…fuck me. Harder…harder," she yelled. If her neighbors didn't have a clue before, they surely had one now.

His thrusts were faster, harder, his abdomen loudly smacking and pounding against her opened legs. He couldn't hold back any longer. He moaned with each powerful thrust into her abdomen.

He collapsed on top of her, panting like a thirsty dog.

"You haven't lost it, babe," she smiled.

"You're still loud as hell," he retorted.

"You shouldn't fuck me so damn good."

"Damn, Cass, why are you so loud? Your neighbors probably think somebody's killing you over here."

"Shit, I know they aren't going to do a damn thing. Their headboard bangs against my bedroom wall every night," she laughed. "That shit is like clockwork. I wait until after their marathon fucking before I go to bed."

Jay laughed. "I know that's right. There ain't nothing worse than listening to someone else getting their groove on and you can't do nothing about getting yours."

He rose up and pulled backward, sliding out of her. His eyes widened. "Ut oh."

"What's wrong?"

"You are on the pill, right?"

"Hell no I ain't on no damn pill. What's the matter?"

He looked down at his limpness. "I lost the condom."

"What do you mean you lost it? Is it still in me? Get it out!"

He raised his hands in the air. "I can't do that."

She rose up on her elbows. "What?"

"Cass, I can't go digging in your twat."

"Oh you're being foolish." She slid her index finger and thumb inside her pussy. She felt around before grabbing the rim of the condom. "I don't know how," she grunted, "you could let this shit happen."

"It's your fault," he said, watching the fishing expedition for the missing prophylactic.

"Damn, it is way up in there too," she said, slowly pulling it out from her insides. Once out, she held the condom up to the light. "It is empty, Jay. Damn!"

"It must've come off before I came."

"You came inside me?"

"Yeah, I guess. I thought the condom was on, Cass. Look, it ain't no big deal. If you get pregnant, I won't leave you hanging."

"Fuck getting pregnant. I don't want to catch a damn STD or worse, AIDS!"

"I'm clean. You have no worries." Jay dressed and headed for the door.

"Where are you going? You're just going to fuck me and leave?"

"Yeah, I'll holler at you tomorrow. Don't forget to take care of your end."

"Yeah, don't worry." Cassie was disgusted. *Damn, why do men do that shit? Fuck and run.*

Chapter 5

Muscular and deeply chiseled, his arm shot out and hooked around her. A foolish little thrill trembled in her belly at the easy strength of him when he pulled her over and under him.

"I have to pee."

"It can wait a minute." His mouth took hers so that thrill twisted into a deep, wonderfully aching throb that extended down between her legs.

"I can't," her breath caught. "I can't hold it."

"Yes you can." Nuzzling her neck where her pulse pounded, he cupped his hands around her hips. "You're all fuzzy and warm in the morning."

Placing her hand on his forearm, she exuded a high-pitched, schoolgirl giggle. "Come on, baby, I have to go. It's not fair," she laughed, his fingers roaming up and down her sides, tickling her. "You're going to make me pee on myself."

Grabbing her wrists, with a devilish grin dancing across his face, Chas pulled Jo's hands above her head and pinned them against the headboard.

Giggling, she went with the flow. "You are always up to no good."

Grinding pelvises to the beat of their hearts as his gaze, as soft as a caress, appraised the curvature of her lips, the Asian slant of her eyes—odd for an African American woman with not an ounce of Asian in her bloodline—and her button nose that reminded him of Rudolph the Red Nosed Reindeer, especially when she laughed uncontrollably. Her alabaster skin, with a hint of amaretto, was flawless, smooth as silk and always remained flustered-like.

Releasing his hold on her wrists, stroking a gently growing fire, he scooped his hands under her hips, lifting them, as her thighs willingly inched apart as he slid inside her. Deeper inside her, she released the tension her muscles had around his straw, allowing him to stir deeper into his favorite drink.

Grinding inside her, his hips moving in circles as if silently fucking her to a salsa beat, he kissed her and said, "You like that, don't you?"

Unable to speak, she nodded, his steel drilling deep inside her cave, hitting against the back wall of her vagina.

Nestled in her neck, Chas stroked his tongue up to her ear and moaned, "Damn, babe, you got some good ass pussy."

Closing her eyes tightly, Joe tightened and released her muscles around his masculinity, as she tweaked his nipples. "You got some good ass dick, Daddy."

Grunting from deep within, "Is it mine?"

Smiling, Jo nodded her head and concentrated on tilting her hips just right, so his shaft would stroke against her pleasure zone. Immediately, a sensation shot throughout her, causing her to tighten up around his dick. Her delicious and drenched core grabbed a hold of him something fierce.

"Yeah, that's it baby, give it to me," he encouraged, beads of sweat pouring down over his forehead, dripping onto her face. "Fuck your man, baby. Take your dick!"

Biting down on her lip to stifle her outcry, legs wrapped around his waist, puncturing her nails deep in his back. "Yes," she cooed, "right there. Don't stop, baby, right there." The swerve of her hips met his quick, but gentle pounding.

No matter how she tried, she couldn't hold back the tears brought on by the sweet, passionate sensation of his love connecting her. And, at that moment, he whispered, "I love you, baby," giving permission to love him back.

Whispering, "I love you too," in his ear, their bodies erupting in combined, powerful orgasms.

Rolling over onto his back, Chas pulled Jo into him and snuggled into her bosom, planting soft kisses on her nipples.

"I still have to pee." Jo playfully pushed him on the forehead and sat up. Placing her feet on the floor, she used both hands to push herself up and walked to the bathroom.

Smiling, Chas watched her full bottom sway from side to side, with much emphasis because she knew he was watching. Once the door closed, Chas grabbed hold of her pillow, sniffed and closed his eyes, enjoying the after effect of the hardest ejaculation he'd ever had. So hard, his head was pounding.

"Babe, can you bring me an aspirin?"

When the toilet flushed, Jo turned on the shower and then opened the door. "Sure, you okay?"

Cupping his body against the queen-sized pillow, he nestled his head in the pillow and stuck his thumb in his mouth. "No, I need doctoring," he said, in the whiniest voice he could muster.

Chuckling, Jo smiled to herself. "You're such a big ass baby. You feel like Stonefish Grill?"

Nodding, Chas tucked the pillow beneath him. "Sure. Wake me when you get out of the shower."

"I won't be that long."

"Okay, then my nap won't be that long."

Knowing what Chas was implying, Jo smirked and closed the bathroom door. So what if she took long showers? If more people took longer showers, there would be less funky people in the world, she thought to herself, climbing into the shower.

Chapter 6

It was after one in the morning before Raven regained consciousness. Her head throbbing with the kind of ache she'd never felt before, it was painful to open her eyelids. Feeling heavy, like weights were above them, her body spun dizzily, much like the teacup ride at an amusement park. As bile from the pit of her stomach pushed its way up through her throat, she clung tightly to the rim of the toilet and tried pulling herself upward, with all of her might. The nausea rose in her throat and the acidity of the liquid anger tickled her tonsils, causing her to vomit. With her head hung over into the toilet, she regurgitated until her heaves turned dry. Pressing the back of her hand against her lips, she pulled up to her knees, all the while fighting off another bout of nausea.

"Oh God," she whimpered, as welled tears danced around the rims of her eyes.

Falling backward, her back crashed against the wall. The drops burned in her eyes as she stared down at the bloodstained floor. Gently licking her lips, tasting the dry, crusty crimson that formed around the edges of her mouth, she tightly closed her eyes. All thoughts immediately returned to the pounding inside her head, causing her to lean her head back against the wall.

During the next three hours, Raven lazed around on the bathroom floor, attempting to regain her since of stability. Deafening was the pounding inside her head. Pulling her knees into her chest, resting her elbows on her knees, grabbing her head and twining hair through her fingers, she tightly pulled strands of hair, hoping to relieve the pain that had taken up residence in her head. Streaming down her face, hot tears made tracks through the dried, crusty blood around her mouth. Squinting, she tried to shake her blurred vision. Swollen lips felt like they had been injected with an overdose of Novocaine, as her face ached, afraid to move. Terrified, she was finally reaping what she'd been sowing for years. For the first time in her life, she felt alone, abandoned.

Holding her breath, she endured the pain of reaching above her head, grabbing onto the sink and slowly, but painfully, pulling herself up. Holding up her head, she looked into the mirror, gasping at the black and blue vision.

Leaning down, she turned on the cold water faucet and planted her feet firmly to the floor, her equilibrium gone. Wiggling her fingers in the stream of water, she cupped her hands, caught a handful, and splashed it on her face. Her shivering nakedness was limp and heavy, unable to hold her own weight. Looking in the mirror again, Raven closed her eyes and thanked God she was still alive.

Turning off the faucet, her hands tightly affixed to the sink, Raven turned toward the door and proceeded with caution. Once she loosened her grip, she extended her arms before her, using them as guides. Inside her bedroom, she stumbled over to the nightstand, tumbling on the bed before reaching to remove the phone from its cradle. Focusing her eyes on the keypad, the phone rung, startling her. Unable to read the Caller ID, she pressed the talk button and held the phone against her ear.

"Hello, Raven?"

Congo drums playing in her head made it difficult to decipher the caller's voice. "I need help," she whispered into the mouthpiece. "Please, help," her voice trailed off. Falling over to her side, Raven's arm went limp and hung over the side of the bed, dropping the phone to the floor. Cassie's voice resonated through the headset, although unheard.

Hurriedly, Cassie slipped on her shoes, grabbed her purse and snatched her keys from the foyer table, as the door slammed behind her. Seeking revenge escaped her as she darted toward the elevator. Her moral obligation to help those in need overcame, as she repeatedly pressed the elevator's call button, with thoughts of horror streaking through her mind. What was she doing? It was because of her that her beloved Marcy was dead. Because Raven was hell bent on seeking vengeance on Jay, Marcy was the catalyst, used and abused, led astray, resulting in bathing in a pool of her own blood after slitting her wrist. The thought of

Cassie alone, in a cold porcelain tub, crimson rapidly draining from her veins, riddled Cassie's insides with guilt. She should have protected her more. Marcy was weak, unable to defend herself against the Raven's and Jay's of the world.

Vengeance on Raven set aside, Cassie continued pressing the elevator's call button. "Come on, damn it!"

As the elevator descended, remembering she had retrieved Morgan's number from doing a ZabaSearch.com a while back, and rushing toward her car, she pulled her cell from her purse and flipped it open. "Shit," she panted, snapping the phone close, after the recorded message announced that the number had been changed. She decided to call 911, but thought against it. Suppose Raven had overdosed on drugs or something. Hell, Raven was too arrogant to commit suicide. She'd wait until she got there to assess the situation. However, until then, she would continue calling Raven.

After the fifth try, she could barely make out the muffled voice. "Raven, it's Cassie, honey. Are you okay?"

Lying dazed on her back, Raven swallowed hard, her throat dry as the sands of Nevada.

"I'm worried about you, sweetie. I'm on my way, can you open the door?"

Raven nodded and uttered a slight, inaudible moan.

"Honey, can you open the door?"

Languishing, Raven was able to muster sound, although barely audible. "Yes."

"Good, sweetie, I'm on my way. Start making your way to the door. Crawl on your knees, Raven. Do you understand me?"

"Uh huh. . ." Raven's voice was fading fast.

"Okay, I am going to stay on the phone with you."

Rolling over toward the edge of the bed, she tumbled onto the floor, landing on her shoulder. Crying out, Raven tossed the phone and grabbed her shoulder. "Oh," she cried.

Yelling blared from the mouthpiece. "Hello! Raven, are you all right? Answer me, girl!"

Struggling, she stretched her arms, as far they would go, her fingers wiggling toward the phone.

"Raven, you're making me nervous and very worried about you. Talk to me, girl!"

Arching her neck off the floor, she swallowed hard and attempted to speak, but words wouldn't come. Raven wanted to say something. She wanted to call out for her sister, tell her how much she loved her and how sorry she was. She wasn't sure what it was, but it didn't matter because she could no longer speak. Closing her eyes, she suddenly, vividly saw the flying white unicorn and Morgan astride it, horse bucking in the clouds. A solitary tear inched from beneath her closed eyelid and fell to the floor.

Frantically, and finally, Cassie dialed 911. Arriving at Raven's apartment complex, the paramedics were there, along with the men in blue, ramming in the front door.

Someone turned her over. Raven looked up at Cassie who stood behind the paramedic. Cassie was calling out, "Sweetie, can you hear me?"

Remaining motionless, her eyes wide as if she'd seen a ghost, she was terrified.

"Honey, if you can hear me, blink your eyes."

Blinking frantically, she wanted to cry out for help, but someone was breathing into her mouth.

"Miss, are you on any medication?"

Looking at the paramedic, Raven shook her head from side to side, her brows drawing together.

"Okay, can you speak to me?"

Closing her eyes tightly, she slightly opened her mouth. The shrill sound that escaped her was like the cry of a wounded animal.

Chapter 7

"Standing in church at my father's funeral, I didn't know what would have satisfied me more; being ushered into a small cell or staring down at his dead, perverted corpse. Even at his funeral, I felt no sympathy. All I felt was anger. So much so, it took all I had to keep from tossing over the coffin."

John's eyes widened. "Wow, babe, you really need counseling, you know? I'm sure there are groups that hold sessions to discuss this kind of thing. You're not alone, I'm sure."

Shaking her head, she tilted it back, as a tear escaped.

Reaching for her cheek, John used his thumb to wipe away her pain. "Baby, I am so sorry you had to endure that."

"When I was eighteen, I had reconstructive surgery."

As much as he wanted to, John was finding it difficult to sit and listen to the woman he loved, talk about being repeatedly raped by her father.

"He tricked me out too."

Gasping, John's face fell into the palms of his hands. He wanted to cry for her, take her pain, ball it up and toss it far away where it would never affect her again. Unfortunately, life isn't that easy.

Wordlessly, she stared off into the distance. "You know, I always wondered what I had done to make him hate me so much…"

"It's not your fault, Deborah." Seething with anger, John spoke between clinched teeth. "Your father was a sick motherfucker, and your mother was blinded by it all. She was weak–"

"Was she? Or did she not care that her husband was fucking her eight-year-old daughter?" Her voice raised a few octaves. "She didn't care about that no good son-of-a-bitch fucking me because she didn't want to fuck him! What kind of shit is that, John?" Yelling at the top of her lungs, Deborah broke down into a cry so deep and hard, she grabbed her stomach and bent over, laying her head in John's lap.

Stroking her hair, John poked out his bottom lip, at a loss for words. He didn't care much for alcohol, but that night he felt like helping himself to a gallon of Vodka, nevertheless.

"I don't know how to help you."

"Just listen to me, John. That's all I need, is for you to listen."

"But, I still think you should talk with a psychiatrist."

"Been there, done that, and it did absolutely no good." Pulling herself up, leaning back against the sofa, Deborah kicked off her shoes and crossed her legs beneath her, Indian style. "Those people do nothing but charge you out the ass and don't say shit, just sit there and listen. They claim to understand how you feel, but how can they? How can they know how I feel if they've never been fucked by their daddy?"

Cringing at her words, John wished she wouldn't be so crass, but then again, he completely understood. However, crass on a woman wasn't cute, even if she was five-foot-three, the color of warm caramel on a sunny day, with pouting lips and hips for days.

Shaking her head, she spoke sternly. "No, there is absolutely nothing a shrink can do for me, except drain my damn checking account."

"I could really use a drink; how about you?"

Chuckling, Deborah leaned back and glared at John. She knew her confessions were getting the best of him; she loved him more for sticking with her. He could have easily turned on his heels and hauled ass, instead of deal with a basket case.

"Oh, you drink?"

"I do now," he chuckled, shaking his head, and resting his hand on her knee. "I have a bottle of Patron Chas left here a few weeks ago."

Hunching her shoulders, she smiled. "Sure, why not. Maybe I'll drown myself in it."

Returning with two glasses, and the bottle of Patron, John sat beside Deborah and poured them both a glass, filled to the rim.

"Honey, I think they are supposed to be shots."

Raising the glass up, he assessed it and declared, "Consider this a mega shot."

Deborah smiled, held up her glass and toasted. "Here's to us getting fucked up!"

"Here, here!"

Simultaneously, they pressed the rims of the glasses against their lips and tilted their heads back. The Patron flowed down the backs of their throat, stinging hers and stimulating his.

Positioning upright, Deborah yelled, "Whoa," at the top of her lungs, before slamming the glass on the table. "Shit!" Turning up her face, she felt the Patron warm her insides.

Rubbing the back of his hand across his lips, John chuckled at Deborah's reaction and held up the bottle. "More?"

Chapter 8

Was her mind playing tricks on her?

Stepping away from the sink, Raven bent down and looked under it. The pipe, which came out of the floor, was no more than three inches in diameter. It was not big enough for an arm. Besides, it made a severe bend at the place where the sink trap was. So, what was it attached to?

Straightening up, for one alarming moment, Raven felt her head might detach from her neck and float away. It couldn't be the codeine, the doctor at the Emergency Room prescribed for her, could it?

Stepping in closer, she looked over into the sink and saw it again. There it was. Blinking several times, she couldn't believe her eyes. Something resembling the thin tail of a rat was moving around in the drain of the sink. Turning on the faucet, the thin appendage slapped around like an eel, fresh out of water. She jumped back and yelled out for Cassie.

Startled by Raven's outcry, Cassie ran down the hall to the bathroom. "What's wrong, Raven?" Out of breath, she held tightly to the bathroom door.

Looking away, Raven pointed at the sink. "What is that in the fucking sink?"

Looking over into the sink, Cassie looked at the running water and turned up her lips. "Well, looks like water to me, but I could be wrong."

"No, in the drain. What is that shit in the drain? It looks like a rat's tail."

"A what? Okay, you are doing some serious hallucinating."

"Look in the damn sink, Cassie!"

Appeasing Raven, Cassie approached the sink, and looked in. "I don't see anything." She stepped to the side and looked at Raven. "How much of that codeine are you taking, sweetie?"

"Oh stop! Don't fucking patronize me, Cassie. I know what the hell I saw."

"Well it must have drowned." *Next it's going to be a mirage in the fucking desert*, Cassie thought as she placed her hand in the small of Raven's back, guiding her out of the bathroom and into the hall. "Want some lunch?"

"I'm not going crazy."

"No, but painkillers tend to have that affect on a person."

"I haven't had peanut butter and jelly in a long time."

Walking down the hall toward the kitchen, "PB&J it will be," she said, motioning Raven toward the sofa. "Have a seat and rest yourself."

In the kitchen, Cassie prepares lunch. "Have you spoken with your sister? I'm surprised she hasn't been here, considering how close you two are."

Raven remained silent.

Standing in the doorway of the kitchen, with the jar of Jiffy peanut butter in her clutches, and unbeknownst to Raven, Cassie watched her like a hawk; searching for answers to questions she had not yet formed.

Raven felt peering eyes burning a hole through her, so she turned toward the kitchen and gazed at Cassie. Raven knew she wanted an answer to her question; she wasn't sure if she wanted to respond.

"My sister isn't speaking to me right now."

"Why not?"

"Where's my peanut butter and jelly sandwich?"

"I see, don't want to talk about it, huh?"

"Right."

"Well, if you ever want to talk about—"

"I appreciate that, Cassie, I really do. But if you don't mind, I'd like to keep my business to myself."

Squaring her shoulders and standing erect, offense slapped Cassie square between the eyes. "Well, excuse me, Raven, I was only—"

"No apologies needed. I'm just funny when it comes to my personal business."

Jessica Tilles

Paralyzed and unable to tear her gaze away from the back of Raven's head, Cassie questioned why she was there to begin with. Raven was the most unappreciative, self-centered, bitch she'd ever met in her life, and she deserved everything coming to her, so she believed. Was she that cold to Marcy, leaving her to die in her own pool of blood? *What in the fuck am I doing here, fucking with this ungrateful asshole?*

Gathering herself with a deep breath, Cassie sat the Jiffy on the counter and walked toward the closet, retrieving her coat and purse. Slipping into her coat, she had a change of heart. When she opened the door, she looked over her shoulder. "I'll let you get your rest. I'm still having the party, would love to see you there, sweetie." Her moral conviction and obligation followed behind her, leaving Raven to her pitiful lonesome self.

Unusually warm for the month of December, Raven raised the window and inhaled deeply. She hadn't felt fresh air in her lungs since she left the hospital. Sitting in the chair next to the window, the wind flapped the curtain in a cloud above her. A sharp pain rippled across her midsection and for a moment, she was gripped by terrible panic, causing her to bend over in excruciating pain. *Is it time for my period? My cramps have never been this bad before.* After holding her breath and willing the pain away, the cramping ceased in her midsection, but the pain of loneliness was deep and unbearable.

Standing to her feet, she wrapped her arms around her, like her personal straight jacket, and paced the small, but quaint, living room. Who was she fooling? She knew she fucked up by sleeping with her sister's husband. How she was going to correct the transgression, she didn't know. Crossing over that yellow line of danger, she knew there was no way Morgan would forgive her. Standing before the window, gazing out at the bumper-to-bumper rush hour traffic, whisking up and down Interstate-395, she shook her head. If she were Morgan, she wouldn't forgive her either.

Walking into the kitchen, coming to terms with what she must do, she picked up the phone and called Morgan.

The number you have reached, (301) 555-2695, has been changed to an unpublished number.

"Damn it, I forgot they changed the number." Raven leaned against the counter and searched her conniving mind. "All right then. If the mountain won't come to Mohammed, then Mohammed will go to the mountain."

Grabbing her keys, she headed toward the door, but first she had to detour to the bathroom. The closer she got to the bathroom, with each step, the more hesitant she became. Inside, she stood on her tiptoes and peeped over into the sink. Seeing nothing, she released a sigh of relief, pulled down her pants and released herself. Reaching for the toilet paper, she heard a slight flapping sound in the sink. Her body stiffened, cutting off the stream of pee. Her heartbeat quickening, her body slightly shivered with a recognizable fear.

"Stay cool, Raven," she whispered to herself.

Slowly rising, she dropped the used paper into the toilet and flushed it, watching the tiny current of water turn into a miniature whirlpool winding around the bowl, eventually exiting toward the city's popular funky wasteland, Blue Plains. She pulled her pants up around her waist and stood erect. Squaring her shoulders, she tightly closed her eyes, praying the annoying, yet fearful, noise away. Facing the sink, she took one-step closer and leaned over. The black thin tail of the rat flapped around, feeling the cold porcelain. Quickly jumping back, she ran to the pantry and grabbed a gallon of bleach. Darting back to the bathroom, she stood in the doorway.

"Get out of here," she yelled, "get out of my fucking sink!"

Head spinning and hands shaking, her nerves got the best of her. She struggled with the childproof top, before splattering bleach everywhere. White dots immediately appeared on her navy blue cardigan. Taking two steps toward the sink, she leaned in closer. Peering down, the tail was still flapping around, making a nuisance. Pouring the bleach down the drain, a loud squeaky shrill consumed her head, before the tail disappeared.

"Stay out, you little stinky fucker!"

Grabbing the towel from the wall rack, she jammed it into the sink, clogging up the drain. She quickly changed before leaving the apartment.

Chapter 9

Nestling Franklin gently into her bosom, Morgan closed her eyes and dozed for a few hours. Mentally stressed and drained, the only source of comfort was Franklin. He loved her unconditionally and, fortunately, was too young to know anything about his disgusting aunt and spine-lacking father. As much as she tried, she couldn't get to sleep, her mind racing at warp speed, wondering what she would do next. Truth be told, she loved her husband deeply and wanted him back in their bed, more than she was willing to admit.

Opening her eyes to a peaceful Franklin, Morgan kissed him on the forehead and climbed out of bed. Building a fort of pillows around him, she gazed down at her baby. He was beautiful, in every sense of the word. She smiled at his tiny hand, fingers, and toes. Leaning in, she kissed him again, inhaling his innocence before turning on the baby monitor sitting on the nightstand.

Tightening the belt around her robe, she heard Arthur scurrying around downstairs in the kitchen, when he should be at the office. A part of her felt awful, the way she treated him the day before. As much as she wanted to hate him, she couldn't do so. It wasn't in her heart to have hatred for anyone, even her sister. It was in her heart to forgive him, and she planned to do so, but in her own time. He was going to suffer for his indiscretion. How long he would suffer, she didn't know. Maybe until she no longer hurts.

Descending to the bottom of the stairs, she looked around the foyer and noticed the accumulation of dust, before proceeding to the kitchen.

"You're not going into the office?"

Arthur shook his head and continued rummaging through the drawer. "I'm taking a few days off."

"What about your patients and what are you looking for?"

"Willis is my backup and I'm looking for…" He slammed the kitchen drawer in frustration. "I'm looking for…" Disgust danced over his flushed face. "I'm looking for my damn marriage!" One hand propped on his hip, the other holding his weight against the counter, he stares into Morgan's eyes. "I am looking for my marriage and I can't seem to find it. Do you know where it is?"

Looking to the left, Morgan briefly closed her eyes and pursed her lips.

"I can't stomach losing you, babe." His words were like an arrow, its tip filled with remorse, piercing her heart.

"I don't know what to tell you, Arthur."

"Try, honey, please, try. We can work through this, Morgan." Walking up to her, he took her hands in his and caressed them.

"You and me, we've been through a lot; we overcame. What we have is strong, babe."

What we have is strong, babe. He must be kidding me. Tightening the grip on his hands, she leaned in closer and peered into his eyes, trying to find the soul of the man she would give her life for. "Arthur, if what we have was so strong, then why did you have a relationship with my sister?"

Arthur's lips parted, as if to speak, before she stopped him. "I love you, Arthur. I've never stopped loving you. I just don't like you right now."

In his heart, Arthur smiled. She had confessed she still loved him. There was still hope. His face softened.

Noticing his relaxed composure, Morgan unclasped his hands. "Don't get relaxed. I love Franklin more. I'm doing this for him. He needs his father."

Slightly stunned, Arthur was certain there was still a slither of hope. Deciding against pushing it, Arthur opened the refrigerator and looked in. "Would you like a glass of orange juice? Are you hungry? I could fix–"

"No, I'm not hungry and I don't need you to fix me anything," Morgan snapped. Moving toward the dishwasher, she opened it and pulled out a clean glass. Motioning Arthur to the side, she opened the refrigerator and retrieved the carton of orange juice.

Arthur looked on, a corner of his mouth pulled into a slight frown. "I offered you orange juice and you said–"

Forcefully, she slammed the refrigerator door shut. "I can get my own goddamn orange juice."

Angrily, Arthur lunged toward Morgan and snatched the glass of juice from her hand, flinging it across the kitchen, where it smashed against the wall. Realizing his anger and frustration, he clasped his fingers over his head, leaned against the counter, and rocked back and forth. Tears poured down his face, dripping into a tiny puddle at his feet.

"I don't know what else you want me to do," he sobbed uncontrollably.

Looking into her eyes, desperation danced over his face, as his arms flew out before him in despair. "You've done everything but nail me to the cross, Morgan."

Desperately wanting to be held in his woman's arms, and knowing it wasn't going to happen, Arthur squared his shoulders and inhaled deeply. Walking toward the kitchen door, he looked over his shoulders and said, "If God has forgiven me of my sins, why can't you?"

Looking away from him, she pouted her full lips and pondered his question before turning to look him square in the eyes. "I'm not God."

Her words stole his breath away, his feet heavily planted to the floor, trying to maintain a steady balance, tears welled in his eyes. "You are a child of God and you should—"

Interrupting his thoughts, the doorbell rang to the tune of *Yankee Doodle*.

Chapter 10

Pressing the doorbell, Raven stood outside the massive double oak doors and held in her breath, as if she had a serious case of the hiccups. Cold feet got the best of her. Turning on her heels, to quickly dart back to her car, the massive doors flung open, and stopped her in her tracks. Slowly turning around, she came face to face with Arthur. As the old saying goes, if looks could kill, she'd be dead.

Trying not to choke on her words, Raven managed to push out a fragile and shaky "Hello," before looking down at her feet.

Her unwanted presence added fuel to the fire that blazed deep inside of him. "What are you doing here?" He spoke in a grudging voice.

"How are you, Arthur?"

"What are you doing here," he repeated in the same grudging voice.

"Well, I wanted–" she hesitated, hearing Morgan's voice calling from behind Arthur.

"Who is it?" Morgan asked, stopping abruptly when she saw Raven.

Raven forced a smile. "Hey, sis, how are you?"

Morgan glared at Raven, then at Arthur and back at Raven.

In a seething tone, Morgan snapped, "What are you doing here?"

"May I come in and talk?"

Morgan released a soft chuckle. "I can't believe you had the audacity to bring your black ass to my house." Pushing Arthur to the side, Morgan stepped out on the porch and walked toward Raven. "Haven't you done enough? You're not wanted here. Get off my damn property, you backstabbing, conniving bitch!"

As their eyes met, icy fear twisted around Raven's heart as tears welled in her eyes; Morgan spewed the nastiest words she could muster, slinging them as hard as she could. Lowering her head in defeat, Raven looked down at the ground and pondered on whether to leave her sister forever or try to make things right.

Reaching out and taking Morgan by the arm, Arthur urged, "Babe, come back in the house. Let it go," not wanting a scene to erupt in their prestigious development of Woodmoore Estates.

Looking over her shoulder, and into his eyes, Raven's hatred for him pierced through him like a dull rusty dagger.

When he spoke again, his voice was tender, almost a murmur. "Not out here, Mo."

"Don't you *ever* put your hands on me again," she snarled.

Raven raised her head and listened intently.

"Morgan," Arthur continued, "can we be sensible about all of this? At least, let's go inside where we can talk."

Drawing back, Morgan couldn't believe her ears. "You want this," pointing at Raven, "conniving little bitch inside the house?"

Arthur drew his lips in thoughtfully. "Morgan–"

Cutting him off, Morgan turned her attention to Raven. "Tell me, how did it feel being me and fucking my husband, huh? Did you love my husband's dick? Tell me, sis, did he yell 'Morgan' as he came all up in your rotten ass snatch?"

Arthur leaned forward and whispered into Morgan's ear. "Listen, enough is enough. If you want to throw insults, fine. However, you *are* going to do so in the house. We will *not* air our dirty laundry for our neighbors to talk about."

Squaring her shoulders, Morgan folded her arms across her breast, and gazed at Raven. "You have five minutes to say what you have to say then I don't *ever* want to see you again." Tilting her head back, she looked up at Arthur. "Five minutes."

Nodding gloomily, he placed his hand in the small of her back.

Stopping, she looked up at him. "Are you touching me?"

His head swung lazily down and shook from side to side. "Sorry."

Following them into the house, Raven closed the door behind them and stood in the foyer. "May I see Franklin?"

"He's napping," Morgan snapped, motioning her into the kitchen. Standing against the wall, her arms folded across her chest, Morgan nodded for Raven to take a seat. "You have five minutes."

In the corner, Arthur stood quietly.

Nearly collapsing in the chair, Raven's knees buckled. Placing her purse on the table, she folded her hands flat on the table and looked at Morgan, searching her heart for an ounce of forgiveness.

Chuckling nervously, "How do I start off," Raven said, staring at her purse.

Pulling the chair from the table, Morgan glared down at her sister as she slowly sat in the chair. She had a lot of questions she wanted answers to. No better time then the present, she thought.

"What happened to Mama and Daddy?"

Raising a fraction, Raven's left brow arched. "What do you mean? You know they died in a car accident."

"Yes, I know." Morgan's words expelled slowly and with vengeance. "Why did you do it?"

Floodgates opened and Raven's memories of that fatal day gushed out of her, taking all her remaining strength with the current.

"Mama and Daddy are dead because of you!"

Biting down on her lip to stifle a cry, Raven shot Arthur a pleading look.

Arthur turned his head in disgust.

Lowering her head, her body slumped over the table as tears forced its way down her face and onto the table. Her mouth opened, but no sound would escape. Shaking her head from side to side, she was forced to contend with memories she had pushed back in the cellar of her mind, never to surface again, until now.

"Why are you doing this to me?" Raven cried.

Propping her chin in the palm of her hand, Morgan felt no remorse for her sister. Gazing at her, she tried to read her emotions. Was Raven putting on an act? Morgan was well aware of her Academy Award-winning performances.

"Raven, if you want to make things right with me, now is the time. You will give me answers to everything I want to know."

Rubbing her eyes with the back of her hand, Raven shook her head vigorously. At this point, she was willing to do what ever it took to get back into her sister's good graces. Morgan was her lifeline. Without her, she felt dead.

Handing Raven an unopened box of Kleenex from the pantry, he felt sorry for her. He could see why anyone would want to be in Morgan's shoes. Not taking anything from his discretions, he was a good catch and damn good husband. Morgan never wanted for anything, and never will as long as he was alive.

"Thank you," she murmured, making a point not to look in his direction. Opening the box of Kleenex, she whipped out a sheet, folded it and caught the tear that had escaped her tear duct.

"Morgan, I was young. I didn't know what I was doing. I didn't think they would get into an accident." Feeling as if she were going through an interrogation, she asked for a glass of water.

Morgan eyed Arthur and he proceeded to get her a glass of water. Placing it before her, he pulled back the chair, opposite Morgan, and took a seat. He was intrigued by what was taking place. Answers to questions regarding events in Morgan's life, events he'd never heard mentioned until now, had his full attention. Besides, the spotlight was off of him and was beaming down on Raven. However, he was sickened at the very sight of her; he felt his insides become a hard knot of disgust and rage. It was because of her he was in such a predicament.

"I know what I did was wrong."

Anxiety got the best of Arthur; he needed to know what she did wrong, so he asked. "You killed your mother and father?"

Quickly, Morgan directed her rage toward Arthur. "What right do you have to question anyone about anything?" She wanted to tell him to shut the fuck up, but she sensed he was at the edge; she wasn't ready for him to jump.

"No, I did not kill my parents. They were in a car accident."

"You put the beehive in the back seat of the car, which upset the hive. While Mommy and Daddy were driving on Texas Avenue, down through Fort DuPont Park, the bees became restless, swarmed out of their hives and attacked Mommy and Daddy, causing Daddy to lose control of the car. It crashed into a tree, killing them both instantly."

Shaking her head, Raven cried like a baby.

"I see it every night in my dreams, Raven! You killed them and I knew about it. And, as *always*, I had your fucking back. The police asked me how the hive got into the backseat of the car and I lied for your no good, backstabbing, trifling ass. Maybe my life would be more at peace had I told the truth. You'd be away in jail for killing your parents and I wouldn't be ready to cut his," pointing at Arthur, "damn throat for sleeping with my sister!"

Besides herself, Raven fidgeted in the chair, sobbing. "I didn't mean for all of that to happen. They punished me and I wanted to get back at them for punishing me. I didn't know they would die."

Morgan hesitated. "That's your problem, you don't think about anything you do. You just do it, without regard for anyone or anything."

There was a long pause of silence, before Arthur peered at Raven's face, his head tilted to the side. "What happened to your face? Your mouth is swollen. Did you do that Morgan?" A slight grin hid behind his sarcasm.

Looking at her face, Morgan said nothing. She noticed Raven's face when she appeared on her doorstep, but knew it wasn't from her. Reaching inside her purse, Morgan pulled out a carton of Newport 100's and a lighter. Sliding the long, thin stick between her tightly pursed lips, she ignited the lighter and inhaled deeply.

Raven frowned up her face and looked in Arthur's direction. The urge to spit in his face overwhelmed her, but she held back her emotions.

"No, I didn't do that to her face. It's obvious that karma paid her ass a visit," Morgan spewed as smoke oozed from her lips.

Raven remained silent.

"Let me say this and then I am done with you. All my adult life, I knew you were the cause of Momma's and Daddy's death. And, more importantly, I knew it wasn't an accident." Tears streamed down her face, her eyes conveying the fury deep within her.

Stirring uneasily in the chair, Raven swallowed hard trying to hold back the tears.

"You meant for them to die!" Morgan's breath caught in her throat as she felt her heart beat rapidly. Every fiber in her body wanted to lung across the table. "You couldn't get your way, so you killed them. You are an evil spirit, Raven. Everything you touch, everyone you involve yourself with, turns to ruins, even my marriage."

Warning spasms of alarm erupted through Arthur. Morgan's body movement spoke volumes, as she wiggled around in her seat, her hand, once flat against the table, was now bald into a fist.

Biting down on her lip until it throbbed like her pulse, a sensation of intense sickness and desolation swept over Raven. Everything Morgan said was true, she thought, as she slid her chair back and stood to her feet. Grabbing her purse and placing it under her arm, she clasped her hands together, clearing her throat.

"I know what I've done is inexcusable, Morgan. I came here to apologize." She faced Arthur. "I don't think words can convey how I'm really feeling. If you can find it in your heart–"

"Oh, you know about people's heart?"

Mentally, Raven keeled over. Morgan's insults were barbed and hurtful. "Morgan, you have every right to be angry at me. If you hate me, I don't blame you. I know you're hurting. But, I will not stand here while you fling your nasty insults at me. I know what I am and I don't need you to remind me."

Blown away by Raven's change to victim, Morgan abruptly stood up and kicked the chair with the back of her calves. "Who in the fuck are you talking to? You've got some nerve, you hateful bitch, trying to turn the fucking table; acting like you're the damn victim."

Tears slowly found their way down her cheek, as Raven squared her shoulders and stared blankly at Morgan.

Unable to recognize the woman before him, Arthur sat frozen, mouth wide open. What happened to the timid, loving, happy-go-lucky woman he married, the mother of his son? He didn't know this woman, the monster he and Raven created.

Slamming her fist on the table, Morgan yelled, "Get out of my face before I whip your ass again!"

Sniffling, Raven reached for a sheet of Kleenex and wiped her cheeks, before she defiantly smiled at Morgan. "Oh, that will never, *ever* happen again." The animation left her face, because she ached with an inner pain that was indescribable and quite unbearable, but she hid it well.

Morgan slightly tilted her head, gazing at Raven in amazement. She couldn't believe it. Raven walked through her door with an apologetic disposition and now she was back to herself. *Damn, what an actress*, Morgan thought.

"Let yourself out; don't darken my doorstep again. And, if you so much as look at my husband again, I will forget you are my sister and chop your ass up into little pieces, bitch."

Flashing a slight smile, a warning voice whispered in her head. She, better than anyone, knew that Morgan was capable of beating her at her game. After all, she learned everything she knew from Morgan. Looking toward Arthur, Raven almost had second thoughts, but…not happening.

"Brother-in-law, did the opportunity arise for you to tell my sister about Reneé?"

Morgan's head snapped around at light speed, like Linda Pearl from *The Exorcist*. "Who is Reneé?"

Crimson red was the color of Arthur's cheeks, as his mouth hung open.

"Oh you don't know about Reneé?" Raven softly chuckled. "I wasn't sure how I got that yeast infection, but I put two and two together."

Arthur was frozen solid, like a hunk of ice being chiseled and formed into an ice sculpture of an ass.

"Well, it's obvious you and *your* husband have things to discuss. I'll leave you now. Kiss my nephew for me."

Watching Raven sashay from the kitchen to the foyer, her eyes plastered in that direction until the massive doors closed shut. Then, she turned her stare in Arthur's direction.

Chapter 11

Sitting behind the steering wheel, Raven stared blankly at the mini mansion, occupied by Mr. and Mrs. Ward and June Cleaver. *Even after his indiscretion*, Raven thought, *she's still going to forgive him, but she won't forgive me.*

"To hell with you, Morgan," she yelled, slapping the gearshift into reverse, peeling out of the driveway and skidding off toward the security gate. Waving her through, the gatekeeper was familiar with the Carrington's obnoxious sister. "You'll need me, more than I'll need you." She was lying to herself and she knew it. Admitting her indiscretion was going against her belief of accepting responsibility for her actions.

As she tore down Enterprise Road toward Central Avenue, her thoughts traveled to Chas as Alicia Keys crooned Prince's *How Come You Don't Call Me? Good question*, she thought, turning left on Central Avenue heading towards Washington, DC.

Taking the corners of the residential street in Bowie, at forty-five miles per hour, the tires to Raven's Mustang squealed their protest before abruptly stopping at 4506 Truman Terrace.

Feeling her body jostled from sleep, as Chas shifted behind her, Jo scooted and nestled her behind against him. Feeling the heat of his chest on her back, and the intimacy of his touch, she instantly remembered everything about the night before.

Draping his arm over and around her neck, pulling her in even closer, Chas pressed his lips against her hair and softly kissed. "Hey you."

Cooing, she folded into a ball, her behind snuggled against his semi-erect tranquilizer, hoping to be knocked out, once again.

Naked from the night before allowed him easy access, as he wiggled his fingers between her thighs, inching toward her sweet spot.

Wooing, she slowly slithered around on the sheets, parting her thighs. "What are you doing," she moaned. "You are so bad." The smile in her voice and the parting of her thighs was permission to enter. Folding her lip inside her mouth, she gently bit down as he slid his girth inside her zone, providing instant pleasure. "Ah, yes, baby. Mmmmm…"

Muscular and hard, Chas' strokes were deep and intense, for the morning after a night of intense lovemaking. "Tell me," he said, caressing the fullness of her breast, "how do you want me to love you?"

Never been asked that before, she had always thought she wanted this. However, now she didn't know what to say. "Do anything you want." Gurgling when the tips of his fingers connected with her peanut-sized nipples, "Explore me…teach me about myself," she moaned.

Withdrawing his palms to her knees, he pulled them up to her chest, deeply moaning from the tightening around his shaft.

"When you touch yourself," he began, "what do you imagine?"

She closed her eyes. "I'm a three-hundred-year-old mahogany table…and I'm being polished, and the slightest scratch would ruin my value." She licked her fingers and stroked her swelling.

Fluid as a stream of water, his tongue stroked the back of her neck, as she bucked and trembled. "Let it go, baby," he whispered in her ear, bringing chills down her back. His large hand took her face and took it gently, as deep moans escaped him. "Ooh, sweet, sweet, Jo Ann, give me all of your love, lady."

"I want to," she softly cried. "I really want to."

"I'm not going anywhere," he spoke into her neck, his penis fluidly gliding in and out of her wetness. Smacking sounds from his stick stirring her juice surrounded the room.

"I love you," he said.

Like blades of thin grass, the hair on the nape of her neck stood. "I…I," she stuttered, as her body convulsed. Failing past relationships made it hard for her to commit her heart. "I," she hesitated. As much as she cared for Chas, she wasn't sure if she really loved him. Love, a word she never played with or tossed around like a bad weave. "I," she yelled, her body trembling profusely, as he stroked the hell out her, fast and quick.

"You what?"

"I…I," her voice short and bouncing around as if she were running on a treadmill, at warp speed.

Their long strides were evenly matched, as she pushed her ass into his abdomen. "Oooh," she cried out in extacy, as he pumped harder, with the deep intensity he need to feel to explode inside her.

"Uh, uh, uh, uh," he moaned with each powerful thrust. That last "uh," was long and drawn out, escaping from deep within.

Caving in and throwing caution to the wind, she smiled and said, "I love you too, babe." Being with Chas felt like a dream. It all seemed too good to be true.

Rolling over onto his back, Chas stretched his arms out to the side and blew hard pants through his full, succulent lips. "Do you want to know what I think?"

Rolling over onto her stomach, Jo hung her head off the side of the bed, her arm dangling over, fingertips slightly scraping against the carpeting. "A penny for your thoughts."

"You should move in with me."

Body movement ceasing, she raised her head, turning to face him. "Move…in here…with you?"

"You're practically living here as it is. Each day, your clothes seem to move into my closet."

"What would that mean? I'm not living in sin, Chas."

Chuckling, Chas stroked the spine of her back. "Then marry me."

Hopping up off the bed, she danced around the room. "What did you just say? Oh my, God, what?"

Rising up in bed and leaning back against the headboard, Chas smiled. "I love you. You love me. Why not get married?"

"This is so sudden. I mean, we've hardly–"

"We've been together, every day, for the past three months. Shit, I ain't getting any younger and I want to be married. I'm ready to settle down."

"And you think I am the one to do this with?"

"I *know* you are."

Butterflies flickered around in her stomach, as nervousness took over. "Are you sure, Chas? I mean, you just told me that you love me."

"I've always loved you. I fell in love the moment I saw that cute button nose of yours, the curve of your top lip…have I ever told you how much I love your top lip?"

Chuckling, "you are so silly," she said, slipping into her robe. Tying the belt tight around her waist, her eyes smiled at him.

Standing on the stoop, Raven extended her long index finger toward the doorbell. Before pressing, she took a deep breath. Her last encounter with Chas wasn't the friendliest, and she was sure this encounter would be similar. But, she needed to bring closure to that episode of her life. Pressing her palms flat against her hips, she smoothed them over her hips and pursed her lips together.

Snapping toward the hallway, Jo heard the doorbell. "Stay put, I'll get it, going to brew coffee anyway." Approaching the doorway, she stopped and looked over her shoulder. "Since your proposal was impromptu," she raised her left hand in the air and wiggled her fingers, "when am I going to get my ring?"

"Soon," he smiled, motioning her toward the front door.

Impatiently, the doorbell rang again.

"Coming," Jo sang, descending the steps, opening the door and coming face to face with her co-worker.

Looking like a deer in headlights, Raven looked Jo up and down.

"Oh my God, what are you doing here?" Jo asked, smiling widely. "Do you know Chas?"

Borderline irate, but refusing to let anyone see her sweat, Raven looked over Jo's shoulder. "I guess I don't have to ask you the same thing. It's obvious you know my man."

Though her face remained masked, a glimpse of surprise escaped Jo's lips.

"Your man?"

Impatiently, Raven looked past Jo and into the house, toward the stairs. "By the looks and *smell* of things, I interrupted something."

Propping her hands on her hips, it was obvious Chas failed to tell her about *his girlfriend*, the woman she worked side-by-side with, every single day. *Damn it! I knew his ass was too good to be true.*

Yelling from upstairs, "Babe, who is it?"

"Nobody," his lady yelled quickly, noticing the parting of Raven's mouth.

"You are such the tramp!" Raven snarled.

Maintaining her composure, Jo stepped outside and closed the door behind her. She was all too familiar with Raven's antics and had no plans of being added to her list of victims. "How about we hash this out now, because I have a man to get back to; and, I do believe you are due an opportunity to get what ever it is off of your mind."

Looking around, Raven curled up her lips. "Not here. We can take a drive."

Jo's perfectly arched brow raised. There was no way in hell that bitch was going to get her out and snap on her. "No, we can't *drive* anywhere. We can talk here."

Smirking, Raven pointed to her robe. "Are you sure? The air is chilled."

"I'm fine, thank you."

Reaching inside her purse, she pulled out a cigarette and placed it between her lips, as she looked for her lighter.

"Listen, I didn't know that you and Chas had any involvement."

"I bet you didn't. However, it's obvious to me that you are his past, which is cool. We all have them," she said, looking Raven up and down, "unfortunately. But I would like to know what is going on now that would make you show up at his front door, this time of morning."

"Well, what ever Chas has told you about me. Uh, I assume he has told you about me."

"I'm sure you were an after thought he would've mentioned, one day."

Chuckling, Raven puffed the cigarette and dragged deeply. "I'll let that one slide. You should know not to fuck with me or what's mine." Raven tossed the cigarette to the ground. "Look bitch, Chas is my man. I don't know what he has or hasn't told you, but you've got it all confused. Sure, we had our issues, but we never called it off. So, he lied to your high yellow ass."

Squaring her shoulders, Jo insisted on being the woman between the two. "Your insecurity is not cute. Being jealous is not becoming."

"I'm not jealous. Like I said, we had some issues and I'm here to rectify things."

"So, I guess you standing out here will make him want to have something to do with you? Look, I don't want to argue with you over a man, but I really didn't know anything about you."

Climbing out of bed, Chas slipped into his pajama bottoms and headed downstairs. "Babe, where are you?" Getting no answer, he stood at the base of the stairs and looked around, noticing the door was slightly cracked. Hearing muffled voices; he walked over to the window and peered out. He noticed Raven's car parked in the driveway. "Shit!"

Walking toward the door, he placed his hand on the knob, about to open the door until he heard Jo's voice, in complete control. Stepping back, he sat on the bottom step and listened intently.

Relaxing her posture, Raven retreated. "I'm hardly jealous of you, Jo. I'm much better than that."

"You're not jealous of me, you're jealous of the situation."

"Bitch, please get a fucking grip. You are hallucinating."

"The problem with women like you," Jo began, "is that you don't know a good man when you have him. You lack *no* strength whatsoever. And, for real, if I am fucking him, it's none of your business. But," she said, slowly turning around, "let's just say that I am. What exactly could you or would you do? Nothing."

"I would have to make a decision, now wouldn't I?"

"You don't have that option anymore, Raven. He broke up with you, so he already made the decision."

"Oh, now you're a fucking deaf mute? Didn't I tell you we didn't break up?"

"No, I'm not a deaf mute, Raven, and I won't be too many more names. But, what puzzles me is that you are standing in my face, trying to figure out if I am your replacement."

"I don't have to worry about you replacing me. Call Chas out here, he'll tell you. Right now, you are just a piece of nasty ass for him to get his rocks off. *I* have his heart. Recognize that shit!"

What's the use arguing with this trick? Resigning, Jo backed up against the door and wrapped her hand around the doorknob. "I believe I can speak for Chas when I tell you that you are no longer welcome here. And, you don't have his heart. I do," she bragged while backing into the house. "Oh and there's one more bit of information I'd like to share with you." Pausing slightly to give her words maximum effect, she smirked before administering the ultimate dagger. "We're getting married."

Slamming the door in her face, Jo turned and came face to face with Chas, startled. "Oh, I didn't know you were here."

Lowering his head, he raised his eyes up and looked toward her. "I'm sorry I never told you about Raven."

"It's okay. She's in your past, right?"

"Right, we broke up about a month before you and I met."

"It is okay, Chas. No need to explain," she exhaled and tightened the belt around her robe. "Want some coffee?"

"Yeah, sure," he smiled a sigh of relieve and followed on her heels. "Wow, it is a small world. I didn't know you all worked together."

Facing him, Jo looked to the left and bit the inside of her mouth. "I knew."

Chas shot her a puzzling look.

"You came up to the office once."

"So, when we met at Jaspers–"

Nodding her head, "I knew who you were–"

"And you never said anything."

"I figured you two were no more, since you gave me your number."

Pulling her into him and planting a soft kiss on his favorite part of her lip, the sexy curve of her top lip, "You figured right," he said. "And even though you weren't aware of our history, you stood up for me. That let's me know I got the right one."

Speaking in a low, even cadence, Jay questioned Cassie about Raven.

"She's sick!" Cassie barked. "What do you want me to do, if she's sick?"

"That bitch is too hateful to be sick. What's got her so damn sick anyway?"

Cassie stood and watched Jay pull off his jacket and toss it over the arm of her snow-white sofa. Cringing, she lunged for the jacket and swung it over her arm. "Jay, why do you keep throwing your shit on my sofa?

"Fuck that sofa, bitch!"

Pulling her hand up to her chest, Cassie turned and walked over to her favorite chair and sat down, somewhat hunched over, the jacket resting across her thighs.

"Raven has got to pay!"

"I don't know, Jay. I mean, she's dealing with some demons. She's paying already."

"Oh, so you don't care that she killed Marcy."

Lowering her head, she chose her words carefully. "Raven didn't kill Marcy, she killed herself. Marcy had issues, long before Raven came into the picture. She had issues when you two were together, but you were too busy fucking her brains out to notice."

"Stop taking up for that bitch!"

"I'm not taking up for her; I'm only speaking the truth! It's wrong, Jay...what we're planning. Besides, we'll never get away with it."

"Sure we will, take that bitch and douse her with gasoline, strike the match and watch her ass burn like pig at a roast."

Gasping, Cassie's mouth fell open. She couldn't believe what she was hearing. *What kind of sick, demented nutcase is he?*

"On second thought, burning alive is way too good for that bitch. We should tie her ass up and drag her down I-95 until her head rolls off and..."

"Stop it! Oh my God, you are sick! I can't do that...I won't do anything so heinous. No one deserves that, no one."

Reaching inside his pants pocket, Jay pulled out a crumpled pack of Marlboro Light's. "I knew you would punk out on me."

Lowering her head, eyes plastered to the floor, she extended him his jacket. "You can smoke outside."

Pursed between his lips, Jay lit the rolled up tobacco and took three deep drags before snatching his jacket from her grasp. "She will pay, you can trust that!"

Chapter 12

Stepping out through the sliding doors, Deborah drew the blanket around her. Despite the fact there was a slight chill to the air, they were experiencing the warmest winter in quite some time. It was a clear, crisp night. The bare-limbed trees exposed the backyard of the adjacent neighbor. From her left, she caught sight of a small aircraft, flying low, that might have taken off from Andrews Air Force Base.

Legs draped over the lounge chair, John motioned for her to sit between his legs. As Deborah snuggled back against his chest, he encircled her in his arms and kissed her on the ear. "Are you cold?"

"Not anymore," she cooed. "It's almost Christmas, think we're going to get any snow this year?"

"I doubt it. More rain than anything else."

Drawing in a deep breath of the night's air, she slowly exhaled. The smell of potential rain lingered. "It's so beautiful out here, in your arms."

Smiling, John leaned his head back against the chair and contemplated how to broach the touchy topic of her seeking counseling. His love for her grew deep, but she needed counseling as well. He wasn't sure how much longer he could comfort her, or if it was doing any good. He couldn't help but to wonder if the negative feelings she harbored toward her deceased father, would inevitably spill over to him. As much as he loved her, and contemplated spending the rest of his life with her, he couldn't stomach what he knew would be the inevitable.

Kissing her, once again, on the ear, he nestled his chin in her neck, and ripped out the words impatiently. "Have you thought anymore about what we discussed?"

Curling up her lips, Deborah rolled her eyes up toward the sprinkling of stars. "I love clear nights. Look," she pointed upward, "there's the Big Dipper. Can you see it?"

"Deborah?"

"John, let's not talk about it right now. It's a beautiful night. Okay, baby?"

"When are we going to talk about it?"

"I've done it before and I don't feel any different." She retorted in cold sarcasm.

"Well, let's do it together. I want–"

"Listen," Deborah yelled, jumping up from the chair and walking toward the opposite end of the deck, "what of 'I've done it before' don't you fucking understand?"

Astonished, her words jolted him. Deciding to think before he spoke, he remained silent.

"I mean, damn, get off my back with that shit. I don't know what the big deal is. I was fucked by my father. There isn't a counselor in the free world that can erase that from my life. I just deal with it, John, and so should you. It is a part of me. I can accept it, why the fuck can't you?"

Standing, he dug his hands deep inside his pockets and stared off into the distance.

Facing him, tears glistened down Deborah's cheek. "I don't know what else you want me to do. I deal with it the best way that I can."

Bringing one leg over the lounge chair, John walked over to Deborah and stood beside her, peering into the distance. Perplexed, he wasn't sure how he was feeling at that moment, but he knew now, more than ever, that maybe he was wrong about Deborah. The thought of not having her in his life, crushed him. But, it was becoming clear that she wasn't the woman for him.

Leaning over the deck's railing; he clasped his hands together and studied them. "I need you to leave," he announced.

Breath caught in her lungs, Deborah stared at him in shock. She stumbled on her words. "Are you sure about that?"

Staring at her with indifference, John's silence spoke volumes.

Allowing the blanket to fall and billow around her feet, Deborah swiveled on her heels and sashayed toward the door, before stopping abruptly. "Are you putting me out of your house,

John? If you are, then I am out of your life as well. I hope you understand what you're doing."

Pulling himself upright, John faced her. He was careful, bowing his head for a moment, seemingly in deep thought, before he spoke. "Deborah, I love you deeply. I want you in my life. Either we are going to work through this or we're not. If not, then you've got to go. Don't have time for you to be straddling the fence. One minute, you're gentle, the next your rough. If you want this thing to work, then let's make it work. Shit or get off the pot!"

Vulnerability returning, yet still angry, she wasn't used to hearing his demanding, decisive, definitive tone. "I need time to think about what–"

"No, you don't need time to think. You've had enough time to think about what you're going to do. Either we're going to do this, or we're not."

"But, with conditions?"

"The conditions are, you will love me one hundred percent and we will put effort into really making this relationship work. We'll leave the issues in the past and love each other one hundred percent."

Perplexed, tears overwhelmed her. "Baby, it's not that easy...putting it in the past."

"You're future depends on it."

"My future?"

"Yep. What defines a person's character is after things go wrong in their lives. How they recover, how they heal. How they let it affect them and how they treat other people."

"But, I don't know how to let it go."

"By leaning on me and our love, trusting in me, trusting that we'll work through this together."

Wrapping her arms around her, she shook her head. "My body had been unwillingly invaded, by my father, of all people. How can I trust a man after that experience? My father said he loved me. How could he love me and do those things to me?" Falling back against the door, Deborah slid down to the cold floor of the deck, stretching her legs out before her. "I do love you, John, and I don't want to lose you. This one skeleton will always be in my closet and peek out from time to time."

Sighing heavily, he understood where she was coming from. However, at the same time, he wanted to compromise, but not wanting to revisit what's been going on so far.

Wiping away the tears with the back of her hand, she mumbled, "What are we going to do?"

"Let's find a counselor. I'll go with you."

"I've been down that road, John."

"But have you been down there together with someone that loves you? Are you willing to do that for me? Are we willing to go through this together?"

Looking up, she gazed into his eyes. "I'll do anything for you."

Chapter 13

Chairs lined up against the wall, a table with magazines piled up high and a nurse sitting at a desk, filing her nails and gossiping on the telephone, Dr. Hargrove's office had an eerie feeling, like a throwback from the sixties. Missing was the huge bowl of red and green lollipops.

Sitting in a chair, Raven glared across the room at the skeleton hanging by a wire; all bones and some of the bones make circles and others are straight lines, like the one hanging in the one-room doctor's office in that movie starring Dan Akroyd and Jamie Lee Curtis, *My Girl*. Shaking her head, she wondered how old of a man Dr. Hargrove was. The nurse from the emergency room recommended she visit Dr. Hargrove for a follow-up, since she did not have a primary care physician. She was rarely sick, and if she had ever gotten sick, she would see Arthur for a prescription. Quickly, she turned up her face at the whiff of mothballs that tickled her nostrils. After looking at her watch, she turned her attention to the band-aid covered pin hole received by the worst injection she'd ever received in her life, a couple of hours earlier.

"Make a fist," the nurse said, as she thumped her finger several times on her forearm. "I can't find a vein. Sweetie, do you do drugs?"

Staring at her blankly, Raven snatched her arm from the nurse's grasp and demanded to be poked by someone with experience.

Flipping through the current issue of *InStyle* magazine, Beyoncé cheesed on the front cover. *That's one bad ass bitch*, Raven thought of Beyoncé. Turning the pages and inhaling the many samples of expensive fragrances, she'd thought about slipping the magazine inside her bag, because that was the closest she was going to get to expensive perfume. *Damn, Danielle Steele has a fragrance out.* "Do the damn thing, is all I say," she mumbled aloud.

"Excuse me?"

Eyes glued to the pages of *InStyle*, being her usual defiant self, Raven refused to look up from the magazine. "Nothing, I was talking to myself," she smiled forcefully. *Go back to your gossiping,* she thought. *Ain't nobody talking to your ass. What in the fuck is taking this doctor so damn long?*

Looking at her watch, thirty minutes elapsed and Raven grew more irritated by the minute. She thought it rude of doctor's to schedule an appointment at a certain time. Yet, it takes them well over an hour before they see you. What kind of bullshit was that?

Sighing with irritation, Raven closed the magazine and tossed it onto the coffee table. "Can you tell me when Dr. Hargrove will see me? I've been here for quite some time, waiting, and I'm getting sick of this now."

Interrupting her call by placing her hand over the mouthpiece, the nurse shot Raven an annoyed look, as though she was busy doing her job, gossiping. "He will be with you shortly. They are waiting for the test results to come back. You may leave and we will call you back when they arrive."

"No thanks. I'll wait." Shrugging her shoulders, she looked around the room in irritable exhaustion, noticing she was the only patient in the waiting room.

Twenty minutes later, she was escorted to Examination Room 1. "It's about time," she mumbled.

The physician's assistant tossed a white paper towel robe on the examining table. "The opening goes in the back. Push the red button on the wall when you're ready."

Raven nodded and waited for her to leave the room, before undressing. Slipping off her jeans, she folded them and placed them neatly in the red-orange plastic chair. There was no need to remove her top, since she was in the gynecologist office. After draping the paper towel gown over her slender arms, drawing it together in the back, she climbed out of her panties, folded them and tucked them inside of her pant pocket. Quickly she pushed the red button and scurried over to the examining table. Hopping up on the table, she allowed her legs to dangle, as she scanned the room. She felt a chill. She hunched her shoulders up to her ears and held the position until the chill made its way down her back and out of her body. She was losing the last bit of patience she harbored, so Dr. Hargrove had thirty seconds to start her examination or else she was going to leave, but not before she cursed everyone out for occupying her day.

Entering the room, Dr. Hargrove extended his hand toward Raven. "Ms. Ward. I'm Dr. Hargrove."

"Hi," she replied, a tad bit pissed.

Detecting a slight attitude, Dr. Hargrove apologized. "We were running your tests and I wanted to ensure the testing was done properly."

Feeling like an idiot, Raven hung her head low before turning her head to the left, away from his glance. Her assumptions were right. He was old as dirt and as white as they come. The thought of this old man digging her vagina, made her cringe, on the verge of vomiting.

"So, it looks like you're about eight weeks pregnant, Ms. Ward."

Sitting upright, a jolt of electricity shot through her and knocked the breath out of her. "Wha…what?" Blinking several times, Raven was confused. *He must have my test confused with someone else.* "What did you just say?"

Entering the room, the physician's assistant stood quietly by the sink and handed him a pair of white Latex gloves.

Feeling light-headed, Raven hung her head lower than the current gas prices.

Pulling up the leather-topped stool up to the examining table, he sat down and wiggled his little fat fingers into the Latex gloves. "Lay back and let's confirm that you are eight weeks. I'd like to do a sonogram to make sure that ugly fall you took didn't harm the baby."

Woozy about the head, Raven continued blinking profusely. "Baby...a baby...that can't be."

Adjusting the stirrups, he patted his hands against the cold metal apparatus. You're your feet in here for me please." He looked at Raven intently. "Why can't it? Blood tests are accurate, Ms. Ward."

Staring up at the ceiling, *it can't be*, she thought, struggling to consider her options. Never being in such a predicament, she mustered all the will she could to push the idea out of her head. There was no way in hell she could be pregnant. *That doctor didn't know what he was talking about*, she thought, as she stroked her belly. *Oh God, please. I can't take any more karma.*

Extending two short fingers, his assistant squeezed a glob of KY Jelly. "Alright, just relax, Ms. Ward."

Tightening up her vaginal muscles, she refused to allow his stubby fingers to enter inside her. It wasn't going to happen. No way... "Ouch!"

"Sorry, you were a little tight," he chuckled, standing up, using the back of his leg to push the stool back against the wall.

Pressing down on her abdomen, Raven could feel his fingers poke and prod against her vaginal walls. It made her sick to her stomach. *He has to be damn near ninety years old.* "So you'll schedule an appointment at the front desk for a sonogram. The earlier you schedule, the better."

Closing her eyes, with mixed emotions, she tried to hold back the crystal forcing their way through her lids, down her cheek and onto the white paper towel robe. "Do you feel the baby?"

"You're definitely about eight weeks," he confirmed, pulling off the Latex gloves and tossing them inside the metal trash receptacle.

Nodding in disbelief, Raven thanked him, and dressed. Walking past the scheduling desk and out of the office, there was no doubt in her mind who was the father. Once the door closed behind her, she fell back against the wall. "What am I going to do?" She grabbed her stomach. "Damn it, Raven, you've gotten yourself in deep shit, again."

Chapter 14

Cassie knew something was wrong when Raven called and asked her to stop by. The premonition swept through her like a chill on a summer night, unexpected and unwelcome, making the hair on the nape of neck stand to attention. Noticing the change in Raven's demeanor, and eager to help, she offered a salve. "Nine West has a serious shoe sale going on at Pentagon City," she said.

Looking at Cassie, Raven shrugged her shoulders.

Cassie pressed the issue. "My girlfriend, Darlene, told me that all shoes were fifty to seventy-five percent off, until the end of the week."

"They're going out of business or something?" Raven asked melancholy and not caring in the least.

"Not sure, but let's go and find out."

Sighing heavily, Raven crossed her hands over her belly and shook her head. "No thanks."

Looking down in momentary defeat, Cassie grabbed the remote from the glass-encased square table that looked like a giant ice cube, and flipped through the channels. "Are you going to tell me what's going on?"

Wishing she could explain her mood to Cassie, Raven knew she would never understand. In one hell of a bind, she hadn't the slightest idea how to free herself. And, she wasn't in the mood for someone else to tell her how she should handle her business.

"So you called me over here to watch TV Land?" With a chuckle in her voice, Cassie stood, stretched and yawned. "Girl, I don't feel like sitting in the house. It's so nice outside, when we should be up to our ass in snow and sleet."

Remaining silent, Raven sat with her back to Cassie, staring out the window.

Fingering the rich, auburn locks behind her ear, Cassie sighed heavily with determination as she pushed on. "If you don't let it out, it'll just eat you alive inside."

Disconcerted, Raven crossed her arms and continued glaring out the window.

"Okay, look, if you don't want to talk then–"

"I'm pregnant," she spoke, barely above a whisper.

"You're what?" Cassie heard exactly what she said, but she needed to hear it again.

As if holding raw emotion in check, she breathed in shallow, quick gasps. "I'm pregnant and," she stopped, her chest felt as if it would burst.

"Oh, my God, Raven. Wow, how did that happen?"

Chuckling at Cassie's, undeniably stupid ass question, the tense lines on her face relaxed. "Well, a man and a woman–"

"You know what I mean!" They both fell out with laughter.

Walking over to her, Cassie knelt down beside Raven and caressed her hand. "I don't understand, honey. Most women, when they find out they are pregnant, show some form of excitement."

Eating her up inside, Raven needed to confide in someone. Other than Morgan, who was no longer speaking to her, there was no one else. Facing Cassie, Raven searched her eyes for sincerity, even though she wouldn't know sincerity if it bit her on the nose. "Can I talk to you, Cassie?"

"Sure you can."

"No, I mean, can I confide in you and trust it won't go any further than here?"

Cassie's expression stilled and grew serious. "Sure, honey, talk to me."

Raven's left brow raising a fraction, as her finger wrapped around the dark fabric of her sleeve. "You have to promise me," she spoke slowly, almost demonic.

Nodding, Cassie took a seat on the sofa, next to Raven. "Alright, I promise."

Wrinkling her nose, she shook her head and slightly sobbed. "I did something that was so unforgivable," she paused, looking out the window, "I committed, what some would call, the Cardinal Sin."

Sitting quietly, Cassie leaned back on the sofa, nestled in the mounds of throw pillows and prepared herself for what was about to come next.

Chapter 15

Propped between two queen-sized bed pillows, Franklin studiously watches his mother search through the heap of purses, on the top shelf of the walk-in closet. Smiling, he clasps his hands around his foot and plays with his toes.

Shuffling around in the closet, Morgan pulled bags down to the floor and studied each one. "Where is my Gucci handbag?" Stepping out of the closet, she looked at Franklin. "Now where did Mommy put her Gucci handbag?"

Giggling, a smile as bright as the sunshine lit up Franklin's tiny cheeks, as he cooed, attempting to answer Morgan's question.

"Oh well," she threw up her hands, "the Coach will have to do."

Inside the closet, she neatly returned the pile of purses to the top shelf and realized the location of her Gucci handbag. Raven borrowed it months ago, never returning it. Contemplating calling Raven for her handbag, anger deep inside of her built to rage as her thoughts turned to Arthur. Knowing every inch of her husbands muscular toned body, she cringed, envisioning Raven's chocolate limbs wrapped around his strong back, pulling him deeper into her. Quivering, Morgan leaned against the closet door and slowly slid down to the floor, as hot tears streaming down her face, was taken over by deep moans of heartache. Franklin's playful laughter snapped her back to reality. He was the reason why she was able to maintain through all of the deceit and backstabbing. Loving her unconditionally, she knew Franklin would never hurt her.

Picking up a stray purse and tossing it up on the shelf, a slip of paper fell to the floor, falling face side up. A phone number stared at her.

"Thomas Whittaker," she mumbled, a wide smile graced her face. She dated Thomas Whittaker for all of two days during her separation from Arthur. "My, my, my," she reminisced.

Standing a broad six-two, Thomas was a replica of Morris Chestnut, with smooth dark chocolate, and sweet in the all the right places. His mint fresh breath was what she remembered most, and he smelled good too.

Curiosity got the best of her, as she quickly dialed the number before her nerves gave way to the build up of urine in her bladder. On the forth ring, she exhaled before she heard the deep, baritone voice answer.

"Thomas Whittaker?"

"Who's calling?"

"Morgan Carrington, we met–"

"Yes, Morgan, I remember. How are you?"

Flattered he remembered her; she fell into the high wingback chair and crossed her legs at the ankles. "I'm doing just fine, and you?"

"Blessed and highly favored…" She heard the resounding smile in his voice. It was music to her ears. "What do I owe the pleasure of this call?"

She leaned her head back and said, "I'd like to take you to dinner," before realizing she made a date with someone, she hadn't seen in two years. She surprised herself. Although she was a woman who never had problems going after what she wanted, but when it came to men…that was a different story in itself. "I'm sorry. I don't know what I was thinking–"

"No, no, please. Don't apologize for what's on your heart."

On my heart, she thought. Morgan didn't know much about it being on her heart, but she did know that she was in desperate need to feel the comfort of a man's arms. But considering, Arthur just wasn't the hot ticket at the moment. "Listen," she leaned forward, resting her elbows on her thighs, "I shouldn't have called, but I found your phone number while looking through my purses and, well, I don't know."

Looking over at Franklin sleeping peacefully, she rolled her eyes up toward the ceiling. She was about to get into deep shit, and she knew it. But, she didn't care. For once, she wanted to be unpredictable. Being Ms. Goody Goody was going into the closet for a long while.

"I would love to have dinner with you. When and where?"

Standing, she straightened her shoulders and cleared her throat. "Really?

"Yes, I think it would be great to meet up and reminisce."

"Well, all right then," she paused, thinking of where she could rendezvous with Thomas. "Uh, do you have a favorite spot to eat?"

"Yes, as a matter of fact, I do. There's a nice spot at the Blvd! at Capital Center, called Stonefish Grill. Do you know it?"

"I've never been there, but I've read about it in the *Washington Post*; owned by a brother, right?

"That's the spot. He owns Red Star too, but I prefer Stonefish Grill. If that's all right with you."

"Yes, Stonefish Grill it is. How does Friday night, around eight, sound?"

"Sounds like a date. Shall I pick you up?"

"No," she quickly blurted out. "I mean no thank you. I will be out and about, so I can meet you there."

"Well, Morgan, it was wonderful hearing from you. I'll see you Friday at eight."

"Yes, same here, Tom. Bye."

Leaning against the wall, she gazed over at Franklin, sleeping peacefully. She closed her eyes and said a quick prayer, thankful there was something in her life she did right.

Chapter 16

Remembering how she squeezed her pelvis tight until she reached an orgasmic high in her sleep, "I used to have dreams about my sister's husband," Raven confessed to Cassie.

Cassie turned up her lips and eyed Raven. "Okay, what's so bad about dreaming?"

"They were dreams about me, well, we were fucking."

Softly gasping, Cassie drew her lips in thoughtfully. "It was only a dream. As long as you don't attempt to act on it, you're cool...right?"

Raven slowly turned her head toward Cassie, raising her finally arched eyebrow. "I wish it were that easy."

Cassie stared at her in disbelief. She knew Raven was capable of many things, but she'd hoped she wasn't capable of the disgusting thought currently running a marathon in her mind. "What are you trying to say, Raven?"

Stroking her belly, Raven looked down and poked out her bottom lip. "My baby will be my sister's stepchild and, I guess, my step niece."

"What? You have got to be shittin' me!"

Raven's brow creased with worry. "I wish I were shittin' you." She gently shook her head, unable to believe it herself.

"Well, damn, I mean I'm at a loss for words. How could you stoop so damn low?"

"Don't," she snapped, "don't sit there and judge me, Cassie. I never claimed what I did to be right, but there isn't anything I can do about it now; what's done is done."

"I can hardly see how you can take that kind of attitude, Raven. I mean, do you realize the wedge this is going to place between you and Morgan?"

"It already has. She knows about my affair with Arthur and, honestly, Cassie, I don't know what I was thinking–"

"You weren't, that's for damn sure."

"Listen–"

"No, you listen to me. You're going to sit there and you're going to listen to every damn word I have to say. It's high time you did. Someone should have pulled your ass a long time ago. What you did was downright wrong and unforgivable. Do you not have any morals, convictions, anything? Did you not think about the consequences your greedy action would have on anyone else, specifically your sister?"

Cassie paced the floor in disgust. So heated, she felt like slapping the shit, hell and damn out of Raven, but she decided against it. For all it's worth, a blatant fool she's not.

Tears streamed down Raven's face, as she stared down at the floor. "I know I was wrong. I tried to apologize, but Morgan's not having it."

"Well, fuck, I wouldn't have it either. You fucked her husband. What do you think she's supposed to do, call 1-800-Flowers? If I were her, I would've whipped your goddamn ass."

"She already did."

"You must get rid of it."

Raven scanned her face for the punch line.

"Raven, you can't possible be thinking about–"

"I'm not killing my baby!"

"Adoption?"

"Not an option. I made my bed and I'll lie in it, no matter how hard it is."

Sitting down on the sofa, Cassie clasped her hands, intertwining her fingers. "That's one hard ass bed."

"Are you going to tell Morgan about the baby?"

Raven nodded her head. "I just don't know how."

"Umph, umph, umph."

"Would you go with me?"

"Go with you wear?"

"To see Morgan."

"Oh hell no, I'm not getting in the middle of that there shit, Raven. No can do, sorry."

"Please, Cassie," she paused, standing and walking over to the window. "Believe it or not, you're all I have. I have no friends and," she choked on her words as she peered out the window.

"From the looks of it, you won't have any family either."

Facing Cassie, tears saturated Raven's face. "I can't lose Morgan. She means the world to me. I know what I did was wrong and I'll have to live with that demon. She didn't deserve this suffering from my selfishness."

Thinking back to Marcy, and how she found her in the tub where she'd bled to death, Cassie couldn't believe she was beginning to feel sympathy for Raven. But, she was, and everyone deserved a second chance, even someone as vindictive, spoiled and conniving as Raven Ward.

Although she searched for a plausible explanation, as to why she couldn't get involved with Raven, she hated to admit how much she was cheering for the underdog. "Okay, I'll go with you. I don't know what I'm getting myself into, but I've got your back."

Wrapping her arms around herself, Raven cried hysterically. "Thank you, Cassie. Thank you so much. I can't go it alone anymore."

With the nod of her head, Cassie realized there was no turning back.

Chapter 17

Chas awakened suddenly to Jo nestled under him. Easing his arm from beneath her head, he moved slowly into a sitting position and enjoyed the well-rested feel of his body. He wasn't a big man, yet tall, he always moved gently. Careful not to wake her, he moved slowly to the window to look out at the hazy morning. Two weeks before Christmas, and he had a lot to do, Jo's stirring about redirected his attention to the bed. Smiling, he thought of how much he loved her and realized it had been a week since he proposed and he hadn't told John, his own brother.

Taking his cell phone from the nightstand, Chas crept out the room and down the stairs to the kitchen, carefully not waken Jo; she was sleeping peacefully. The previous night of lovemaking was a marathon compared to their other nights of sexual bliss; heightened sexuality fueled by a new level of intimacy.

Pulling the chair from the table, he lazily fell into it and flipped open his cell phone. As his thumb pressed against the key pad, his dick still tingled from the previous night. *Damn, that woman is gon' wear my ass out*, he thought with a sunshine smile.

"What's up, big brother?" Chas sung into the phone.

"Morning, little brother."

"How ya doing?"

"I can't complain. What's up?"

"Hadn't talked to you in a minute, thought I'd give you call."

"How's Deborah?"

John sighed heavily and, for what seemed like an hour, there was dead silence on his end. "Chas, man, I don't know. I mean…"

"All is not kosher in the Love Land," Chas chuckled. "What's going on with Ms. Master's in Psychology?"

"How much time do you have?"

"Damn, that bad?"

"You have no clue, man."

"I'm listening."

"Deborah's got some serious demons she's dealing with, man. Her pops molested her when she was child; penetration and all."

"What kind of sick motherfucker would do some shit like that to his own child?"

"I know right. If he wasn't already dead, I'd break his fucking neck my damn self."

"Damn man, that's some fucked up shit, though."

"She goes ballistic in the bed."

"Ballistic? What you mean?"

"Once, when I was deep into it, she started choking me and shit."

"Well they say that shit is supposed to heighten the orgasm."

"Trust me, it don't heighten shit. I had to toss her ass off of me and onto the floor. She had a serious grip around my neck. When I asked her about it, that's when she told me about her pops."

There was silence. Chas was at a loss for words.

"I don't know, man. I'm trying to get her to go to counseling, but it's like taking candy from a child. But she finally agreed to go if I go with her."

"Oh, well that's good." Chas tapped his fingers on the kitchen table, his thoughts straying up the stairs toward the bedroom, wondering if Jo had some hidden secrets she has yet to share.

"So, what's up with you?"

"Huh?"

"You called me. What's up?"

"Oh, yeah, well...guess what?"

"What man?"

"I'm getting married."

"To whom are you marrying?"

"Jo. Who else would I be marrying?"

"Jo? How long have you two been together?"

"About four or five months."

John released a hearty laugh. "Trust me, that ain't enough time to get to know someone. Remember, I've been with Deborah for over a year and I'm just finding out about the shit with her pops."

"I love her."

"I love Deborah, too, but—"

"Jo is not Deborah," Chas snapped.

John pulled back, deciding not to lobby against the impending nuptials. "You're right. Listen, just do me a favor."

"What?"

"Have a long engagement, at least a year. That way, her representative—"

Clearing his throat, Chas cut John off. "I hear you."

Retreating, John smiled. "I'm happy for you, little brother. If you love her, I love her too. Besides, anyone is better than that damn Raven."

They laughed.

"Man, she showed up here and she and Jo had words."

"Damn, a good cat fight, huh?"

"Naw, not really, Jo handled her, but I still don't trust her. You know?"

"I hear ya, man, that Raven is one scandalous bitch."

"I can't believe I never saw—"

"Hey, for real, you knew. Hell, she was fucking your boy when you stepped to her. So, it ain't like you ain't know. You just refused to take off the rose-colored glasses, making her look like a bed of roses."

"Yeah well, she's out of my life now. Jo's a good woman, John."

"I'm sure she is. I wish you nothing but happiness."

"Thanks man. I've gotta jet, I'll talk with you later."

Chas showered, dressed quickly and hit the street.

Sitting straight up in the bed, the closing of the front door scared her out of her peaceful slumber. "Chas?" she called out, listening for a response. After hearing the tires to his brand new Corvette skid down the street, a smile warmed her face as she stretched her arms above her head. Falling back onto the pillow, she stretched her legs wide open and stroked her abdomen. Feeling horny, she wanted her man not her fingers.

Reaching for the phone, she dialed Chas' cell phone. "Come back," she whined.

"Good morning, babe. Oh, I didn't wake you, did I?"

"No, but the throbbing between my legs is calling out for you."

Chas chuckled. "Tell Daddy what you want him to do about it."

"Make a U-turn and take care of me."

"See you in two."

Darting to the bathroom, Jo brushed her teeth as she emptied her bladder. Listening intently, she heard the front door closed. "Oh shit!" Chas' new toy is too fast for his own good.

Chas ran up the stairs to an empty bed. "Babe?"

"Yeah, I'm in here."

Approaching the bathroom door, Chas jiggled the doorknob. "Unlock the door and I thought you would be waiting for me to dive in."

"I had to pee. Get naked, I'll be out in a minute."

Loosening his tie, Chas sat down on the bed. The door opened, exposing Jo's naked, voluptuous frame. A beautiful sight to behold, he was even more confident he had made the right decision, asking her to take his last name.

"Okay, why do you still have your clothes on?"

"Come here." He patted the empty space beside him. "Let's talk."

"Talk? Baby, I don't want to talk," she cooed, sitting beside him, draping one leg over his thigh. "I want me some loving." The concerned look on his face startled her. "What's the matter, Chas?"

"I need to know that you've fired your representative."

"My what? What are you talking about?"

Facing her, he cupped his hands around her face. "Baby, I need to know that I am marrying you and not someone you want me to believe you to be."

"Chas, I've exposed myself to you more than I've ever done with anyone."

"You have any secrets you'd like to share with me?"

She shook her head.

"Have you ever been molested?"

Her brow furrowed. "Not unless you know something I don't."

"What about any past relationships that went sour?"

Fear shot through her, witnessing a side of him she'd never seen before. "No. You're scaring me, Chas."

Cradling her in his arms, he held her tight. "I don't mean to scare you, babe. I love you so much. I just need to know that I know everything about you."

"I love you too, baby. And, yes, you know everything. I've been up front with you, since day one. I would never deceive you, Chas. That is not in my nature. I'm too honest, and I can't believe–"

Placing a single finger over her lips, Chas hushed Jo's rambling. "I love you, Mrs. Walker."

Jo smiled and kissed his finger. She liked how that sounded. "I love you too, Mr. Walker."

Pulling away from their embrace, Chas stood up. "We have not set a date yet."

"Well, no, I guess we haven't. When would you like to be married?"

"December twenty-fifth."

"Uh, that's in two weeks, Chas."

"I know. We can have a small ceremony here."

"That's not enough time to send out invites..."

"Baby, invites to whom? All we need are your parents and..."

"But, honey, this is my first time getting married. I wanted it to be special."

Chas sat down beside her and took her by the hand. "And it will be special. I love you and I don't want to wait any longer to make you my wife."

"Well, I guess I better start making plans. I don't have much time, there's so much to do. Wait, how about we get married on New Year's Eve? That will give me an extra week."

Filled with a sense of sweet satisfaction, he kissed her lips. "Perfect."

Chapter 18

Walking into the living room, adjusting his tie, John leaned down and kissed Deborah on the forehead. "Are you ready?"

Sighing heavily, Deborah pushed back from the computer desk. "Yeah, I guess."

"It's not going to be bad and I'll be with you, holding your hand."

"You better," she smiled. "John?"

While snapping the cufflinks on the cuffs of his crisp, starched white shirt, he stepped into the black leather Kenneth Coles. "Yeah?"

"Let's play a game."

"Sure, when we get back. We have to run, babe, we're going to be late."

"Please, John, I need to calm my nerves. It will only take a minute."

Slipping into his cashmere jacket, John shook his head. "You can't avoid it."

"Okay, I'm not trying to. Please, work with me. Okay?"

John nodded.

"How far is it from Dulles International Airport to Miami?"

"Huh? I don't know."

"How long of a plane ride do you think it would be?"

"You didn't ask that, you asked how far."

"John!"

"Okay, I don't know, about four hours."

Falling over with laughter, Deborah grabbed her stomach.

"Uh, it's not that funny."

"You're kidding me, right? Four hours to fly from here to Miami."

Becoming annoyed, in no mood to play games, John stuck out his foot and propped his hands on his hips. "Yeah, that's what I said."

"I say it's going to take at least two and a half hours."

"Okay that's fine. Can we go now?"

Pulling herself up to the monitor, "In a minute," she said, her fingers dancing across the keyboard.

"What are you doing? We are going to be late, playing childish ass games."

"John, you really do need to relax, honey. It's not that serious."

Ignoring her, for the sake of avoiding an argument, John approached her and rested his hands on her shoulders, massaging them. "What are you doing, Deb?"

"I'm searching Travelocity.com to see how long it would take to fly from Dulles to Miami."

Trying to maintain his composure, he couldn't figure out to save his life what any of this had to do with anything. It was childish and foolish and he no longer wanted to play her kindergarten games. "We really have to go, Deborah."

"Ah hah, you were wrong! It's two hours and thirty minutes, just as I said."

John applauded. "Good for you, now can we go?"

Twirling around in the chair, she looked up at him with the look of discontentment. "I don't think I like your attitude."

"And, I don't believe I like your stalling tactic, irregardless of how immature it may be."

"Oh, now I'm immature. What's with the name calling, John?"

Folding his arms across his chest, he glared her. "Why are you so intent on fucking us up?"

"I beg your pardon."

"You are doing everything imaginable, down to playing childish games, to avoid going to counseling. Counseling you agreed to go to. I'm sick of this shit, Deborah. I am up to my ass with this. You have five minutes to make a decision. Either there's going to be an *us* or there isn't."

"I don't do well with ultimatums, John."

"Call it what you want, you now have four minutes."

"Oh you're being ridiculous!"

"Your time is running out."

"John—"

"Three minutes."

"What? You're joking, right?"

"Nope, not joking; two minutes."

"Fuck you, John. You can take that last minute and shove it up your ass!"

"Excellent! You can pick up your things tomorrow. And, as your girl Beyoncé says, in the box, in the back, to the left. I'm sure you can let yourself out. Oh, and please leave your key on the table."

"Go to hell!" she yelled before storming out of the house and John's life.

There was no turning back, she was adamant and so was he.

Chapter 19

After leaving Franklin at Veronica's, Arthur's receptionist for the past few years, Morgan pumped up the radio to calm her nerves. Anthony Hamilton's *Sister Big Bone* had her bopping her head and feeling quite lively. Deep down, she knew she had no business going to meet Thomas, but a part of her sought revenge in the worst kind of way. She was tired of being the mat everyone wiped their feet on; when they got good and ready, especially Raven. Sadness quickly overcame her, at the thought of Raven. She missed her sister, but what she did was unforgivable. Moreover, as far as she was concerned, hell would freeze over twenty times before she uttered one word to Raven.

"Sister big bone," she sang, out of key and completely off pitch. Fingers snapping and popping, sitting at the corner of Arena Drive and Lottsford Road, waiting for the light to change, the glimmer of her wedding ban caught her attention. Turning up the corner of her mouth, she closed her eyes, removed the ring from her finger and placed it in the ashtray. "Can a brother take you home?" Part of her was hoping those would be Thomas' words, except for her being big boned. While she was healthy, she was far from being a big-boned woman. However, she was thick in all of the right places. *Got a tight booty too*, she thought, smiling to herself as she peered in the rear view mirror. She puckered her lips, and then pursed them together.

As the light turned green, and Morgan turned right on Arena Drive, heading toward the Blvd! at Capital Center, track ten of Anthony Hamilton's CD changed her whole mood. *Damn it*, she thought as Anthony crooned, "Oh when you stop..." *and start falling in love*, she thought to herself. "That's my song, but why does it have to come on now when I'm about to commit adultery? Shit!" Desperately needing to change her mood, she switched from the CD to radio. WHUR 96.3 FM was blasting Heather Headley's *In My Mind*. She plopped her head against the headrest and thought about Arthur. She loved him more than she would ever love anyone, but she was finding it so damn hard to forgive him. A smile crept across her face when she thought of how Arthur used to creep up behind her and hump her leg, like a puppy dog, his tongue hanging out of his mouth, panting; or when he used to walk by her, tap her on the ass and say, "Hey, sweetie peetie." Deep down in her heart of hearts, she knew Arthur loved her. She also knew that, while he was a loving, caring and sensitive man, he could also be naive and the perfect victim for someone as devilish and headstrong as Raven.

Pulling into a vacant parking space, in front of Red Star Tavern, the devil was propped on her shoulder, egging her on. Her common sense was nowhere to be found. Removing the key from the ignition, she thought, *it's now or never*. Breathing deeply, she dropped her keys inside her purse; made sure she had her cell phone, in case Veronica called about Franklin, and exited the car.

Unseasonably warm for the week before Christmas, she pulled her jeans up around her waist. They had slipped down around her hips, just a little, thanks to LA Weight Watchers. Immediately after Franklin was born, Morgan was determined to lose the extra thirty pounds of weight she gained during her pregnancy. The chocolate brown wool turtleneck, with gold stripes, blended perfectly with the chocolate brown suede jacket. The brown suede, four-inch, boots were killing her feet. Sitting her purse on the hood of the car, she fished around for her trusty companion, the red bottle of shoe stretch. Bending down, she squeezed more than a quarter size amount on the side of her suede boot, leaving a wet circle. Unaware of her surroundings, when she pulled herself upright, a baritone voice startled her.

"Still looking good, I see."

Facing him, embarrassment flashed across her face like a bright red stop sign. "Oh, um, hey, Thomas," she hesitated. She didn't know whether to hug him or shake his head. While she was horny as fuck, she didn't want him to get any ideas. "How are you?"

Thomas leaned in and embraced her. "It's good to see you again, lady."

119

Morgan's hands hung down by her side, not knowing whether to hug him back. She felt like a complete fool. Finally, she gently wrapped her arms around his waist and closed her eyes. She was scared as shit.

Afraid someone would see them; she broke the embrace and took a step backward. "It's good to see you too," she said, fidgeting with the straps on her purse. An eerie feeling shot throughout her entire being as she looked around the parking lot. Unfamiliar with such a feeling, she quickly turned on her heels. "I'm hungry, can we grab a table?"

He slightly bowed his head and extended his arm in front of him. "After you," he smiled.

Damn, he's still fine, and that smile, shit! Oooh, please give me strength.

Chapter 20

"Damn, man, you're really going to do it, huh?"

Chas shook his head and chuckled. "Yeah, man."

"As long as she's not like that bitch, Raven," Arthur huffed.

"Fuck that broad, and can we not fuck up the night by talking about her ass?"

Arthur raised his glass of Chardonnay and Chas raised his shot glass of Patron.

"Here's to one of us having a loving marriage," Arthur toasted, tears welling on the brim of his eyes.

Chas noticed the tears and took his Patron to the back of his throat. "Whoa!" He slammed the shot glass down on the table. "Whew, that is some shit, man! That shit is stronger than Jose Quervo."

Arthur sipped his Chardonnay and remained silent.

Chas folded his arms on the table and leaned in close. "What's up with you, man?"

Arthur shook his head. He didn't know where to begin. He and Chas had become the best of friends while Chas was dating Raven. He couldn't find the words to tell his friend that he fucked his girl, while they were together, but he knew he had to tell him. He'd rather it come from him, then for Chas to find out some other way.

"Let's get another round," Arthur said, motioning for Terri, the manager.

Approaching the table, Terri flashed her beautiful Colgate smile and batted her eyes at Arthur. "What can I get for you?"

Arthur lowered his head and smiled. She was flirting with him, and he was enjoying it. Since he wasn't getting any attention at home, why not enjoy it while he was out. As long as he didn't cross the line, again, and bed anyone, it was all in harmless fun.

Arthur smiled, flashed his deep dimples, and licked his lips.

Chas couldn't believe his eyes. Arthur's behavior was totally out of character. He interjected before Arthur got himself in deep trouble. "Terri, another round, if you don't mind."

"Sure," she smiled at Chas.

Chas turned his head. Terri's smile was causing an unwanted rise between his legs.

"Uh, honey, let me get a shot of Patron and a JD on the rocks, with a lemon twist."

"Damn, man, you trying to get wasted?"

"Make it a double," Arthur said to Terri.

"You got it. Be right back." As Terri walked off, she put an extra strut in her hips, giving Chas and Arthur an award-winning ass wiggle performance.

"Damn, man, you see that ass?" Arthur said.

"Yeah, but I'm trying not to though. You know how women are. No sooner than I get a good look at that juicy booty of hers, my cell phone will ring. It'll be Jo. I think women have ESP or some shit. They know when a nigga is fuckin' up," he chuckled.

Arthur's smile turned to a frown as he looked at Chas.

Chas frowned. "What the fuck is wrong with you, Art?"

"You know, man, I really do value your friendship."

"Aw, hell, now you're getting mushy one me and shit. What is it man, you dying or something?"

Arthur took a hot roll from the breadbasket and broke it in two. "Right now, I wish I were. It would surely soften the blow of what I have to tell you."

"Look, man–" Chas stopped talking as Terri approached with their drinks.

"Here you go. Anything I can get you two?"

"Thanks, we're cool," Chas responded, not taking his eyes off Arthur. Waiting for Terri to walk away, Chas zeroed in on Arthur.

"Could you stop staring at me like that? You're making me uncomfortable."

"Sorry, but you've piqued my curiosity, with this 'I gotta tell you something' shit."

Raising his head, "Look, man, this isn't going to be easy," Arthur started before stopping in mid-sentence. In a trance, Arthur's mouth fell open.

Chas followed his gaze toward Morgan and Thomas entering Stonefish. "Hey, man, ain't that Morgan?"

Arthur couldn't speak. He couldn't move.

"Who the fuck is that dude with her?"

Arthur closed his mouth and cleared his throat. "I, I don't know who it—"

"Hold up, what's going on, Arthur?"

Taking the Patron to the back of his throat, Arthur raised the shot glass and motioned for Terri to bring him another.

"Look, if you don't tell me what the fuck is going on, I'm going over to ask Morgan!"

Arthur raised his hand in defeat. "Okay, okay. Morgan and I are sort of separated."

"Huh? Sort of separated?"

"Yep."

"How can anyone be *sort of* separated? Either you are or you aren't?"

"I'm not leaving my house and neither is she."

"What the fuck man, y'all sleeping in separate rooms and shit?"

Arthur looked up and focused on various names of fishes on the wall, to keep from looking over at Morgan—Yellow Tail, Lobster, Pompano, Flounder. *What in the hell is she doing?*

Chas looked over at Morgan, sitting in a booth beside Thomas. "They look like fucking newlyweds and shit. I can't believe this, man. What happened, damn?"

Terri sat Arthur's second shot of Patron on the table. Before walking away, Arthur grabbed her by the hand and smiled.

"Arthur, man," Chas warned.

Ignoring Chas, Arthur kissed the back of Terri's hand. "Lovely lady, could you please bring me two more, and make them doubles?"

"Only if you promise to let me drive you home," she teased.

"Darling, you can do whatever–,"

"Uh, that'll be it for now, Terri, thanks."

"Arthur, what happened between you and Morgan?"

Arthur looked over at Morgan and started whimpering. "I don't deserve her."

"Aw, hell, man, come on now."

"I had an unsolicited affair."

"You cheated on your wife?" Chas sat back in the chair and chuckled. "Man, that's not even your M.O."

"I know, man." He took the third shot glass of Patron to head. Holding his head back, he allowed the painkiller to ease down his throat and straight to his heart.

"Uh, let me ask you this, what is an *unsolicited* affair?"

"I didn't want to fuck her man."

"*Okay*, so why did you?"

"She made me," he began crying.

"Ain't no use in your ass crying now, you done already fucked up. But how can a bitch make you fuck her?"

125

"You know how she can be man, persistent and she black mailed my ass."

Chas titled his head to the side and glared at Chas. "Who is *she*?"

Arthur gulped the JD on the rocks and slammed the glass on the table. "Raven."

"Say what?"

"I met this married woman who happened to be the wife of Ramone."

Chas perked up straight in his chair. "Reneé? You messed around with Reneé?"

Arthur, now moving quickly into a drunken stupor, nodded his head.

"Hold up, nigga, you fucked my woman?"

Chuckling, Arthur downed the last gulp of JD on the rocks. "Naw, nigga, yo woman fucked me. Told me if I didn't fuck her, then she would tell Morgan about Reneé. I didn't know what else to do."

"What the fuck you mean you didn't *know* what else to do, nigga?"

"You wanna take me outside and beat my ass?" Arthur slurred. "Hell, you know how conniving and vindictive she is."

"Naw, I don't wanna beat your ass. I'm beyond doing that shit, but I ain't got shit else to say to your sorry, weak ass."

"Raven killed Ramone and Reneé."

"Oh my God." Chas' world as he knew it, for a hot second, turned upside down.

"Karma is a motherfucker. What I did with Raven ain't any different than what you did?"

"What 'chu talking about?"

"Ramone was your boy, right?"

Chas' brow furrowed. "Right."

"You fucked Raven while she was fucking around with Ramone." Arthur laughed, now drunk as hell. "Karma is something. Karma done bit me in the ass real fucking good, and it bit your ass, too. You just didn't know it."

Arthur was right and there wasn't a thing Chas could say about it. Besides, he knew Raven and what she was capable of doing.

"I've gotta good woman now," he smiled at thoughts of Jo, "Raven is in my past. I really don't give a shit who she fucked."

"I told Morgan about it."

"You did what? Why would you go and do some stupid shit like that?"

Arthur shook his head and peered across the room at his wife, dining with another man. "And you know I love my wife. That woman there," he said, pointing across the room at Morgan, "can't do no wrong. So if she feels she has to get back at me, then so be it." He raised his glass up towards Morgan. "You do what you feel you have to do," he toasted.

As Arthur drank from his glass, Morgan looked over in his direction. Stunned, her eyes were plastered on Arthur. Her heart sank. She felt awful.

Chas shook his head at Arthur, Morgan and the entire fucked up situation.

Chapter 21

"I need to go," she said, grabbing her purse and walking toward the door. She quickly glanced over at Arthur and headed out the door.

"Wait!" Thomas called out to her, heavy on her heels. "Wait a minute, Morgan!"

Outside, in the courtyard, Morgan stopped and leaned up against the concrete planter, sobbing. "Oh my, God!"

Catching up with her, Thomas wrapped his arms around her shoulders. "What's wrong? Was it something I said or did?"

Morgan broke away from his embrace and ran toward her car.

Thomas followed behind her. "Morgan, please wait!"

Searching the bottom of her purse for her keys, Thomas grabbed her by the arm and pulled her into him. "What's wrong, baby? Please tell me!"

Leaning into his chest, Morgan sobbed uncontrollably. Feeling strands of snot running stringing from her nose, she was afraid to raise her head. "I saw my husband in their," she cried in his chest.

"I thought you were separated."

"I am, but we still live in the same house."

"Oh I see," he said, stroking the back of her head. "Well, try to get yourself together. We can go somewhere else."

Raising her head, she rubbed her nose with the back of her hand. "You still want to have dinner?"

"Yes, don't you?"

"Well, I don't know. I mean, I don't know."

Lifting her chin with his finger, he leaned in and softly kissed her lips. Morgan closed her eyes tightly. It felt nice, sweet and loving.

"I have a great idea," he said, wrapping his arms tighter around her, and kissing her on the forehead. "I know of a place where we can get some great grilled salmon."

Morgan smiled at his attempt to make her feel better. "Sounds nice," she said, sniffling.

"Excellent. You leave your car here; I'll drive and bring you back after dinner. Okay?"

Morgan nodded in agreement.

Backing the Mercedes S Class out of the parking space, Morgan strapped on her seat belt. "Where are we going to eat?"

"Trust me," he said, patting her on the knee. "You'll love it."

"I'm sure I will, but can you tell me where anyway?"

Thomas locked the doors and headed toward Arena Drive. "My place."

"Your place? Oh no, I can't go to your place. I don't know you like that, Thomas."

"It's going to be fine. I won't hurt you."

"I don't care, turn this car around and take me back to my car."

"Chill out, Morgan. I don't live far. I live on Lottsford Road, not more than five minutes away. Tell you what, once we get to my place and, if you're still feeling uncomfortable, I'll bring you back. Okay?"

Morgan relaxed her nerves and settled back into the seat. "Okay," she said, figuring a man driving a Mercedes S Class can't be all that bad. And, if he lives off of Lottsford Road, then he has a nice house.

When they entered Thomas' house, he shuffled around, turning on lights, and then dimming them. Morgan spotted the buttery soft leather sofa and fell into it, as if it were a cloud she could lose herself on. Out of nowhere, Maxwell crooned *A Woman's Worth*. Minutes elapsed as Morgan fought the urge to close her eyes. It had been a long day and she was whipped. When he entered the room, she sat up and took a good look at his face. She no longer recognized him. He seemed emotionless, regular, sort of an average Joe you'd find in a criminal lineup. "The bedroom's this way," he said.

"I beg your pardon."

"You want to get back at your husband, right?"

"I don't know what you're talking about and you need to take me back to my car."

Thomas stood in front of her and unzipped his pants.

"I have to go," she said, attempting to get up.

"Sit your ass down," he ordered, pushing her back onto the sofa.

"Look, let me the fuck out of here, you maniac!"

His arm rose, shadowing over her. Then his arm came crashing down, curving at full speed and force through the air. His fist bashed against her head. The arm rose again. His fist struck the side of her head, again.

Unzipping his pants, they fell down around his bare feet. Pulling her upward, his dick already hardened. It looked massive and it curved upward like an accusing finger. "Suck it."

Morgan was motionless, before his arm rose again, ready to swing down across her face. Reluctantly, she took his dick in her mouth.

Moaning at the warmth of her mouth, he tossed his head back. "You like that, don't you?" he asked, with an evil grin while drilling in and out of her mouth. "Swallow it deep. Moan for me, let me know how good this dick is." He thrust it farther down the back of her throat, its head pushing against her tonsil, bringing her to the verge of vomiting. "Suck harder, trick, make me come."

Like the Nile River, tears flowed fluidly down her cheeks. Deep-throated cries from deep within escaped her. "Please," she hummed; terrified that he would kill her if she didn't do as told. He continued pushing deeper down her throat. Each time she would slightly back up, he would smack her in the face. When she felt herself choking, she pulled back, his hand affixed firmly to the back of her head. She heard the distinct pull of phlegm from deep in his throat, the pause, and finally the mass of spit hailed from his mouth. A thumb-sized blob hit her cheek.

"You slut!" he yelled, humiliating her even more.

Pulling away from him, she stumbled to her feet and aimed for the door, but he grabbed her by the arm and tossed her down the hallway toward his bedroom. "Please!" she hollered at the top of her lungs. "Somebody help me, please!"

"Shut the fuck up!" He pushed her into the bedroom, closed the door and shoved her, face down, onto the bed. Retrieving the scissors from the nightstand, he cut her jeans from the waistband, down past the crack of her behind.

Morgan desperately cried into the mattress. Afraid of his actions, she lay still, hoping not to anger him more. The inevitable was about to happen and there was nothing she could do about it.

"Quiet," he yelled, "and you better not move either."

Face down, the room was dark, and for a moment, very still. Finally, she heard movement. It sounded like a closet door opening. He reached in, pulled down a small box. Remove the lid, he walked around to the side of the bed, and turned her face toward him. Using his index finger, he scooped a finger-size amount of white sugar looking substance and held it close to her nose. "Snort it." Morgan didn't want to, but she didn't know what else to do. She breathed in. "One more time," he said. She did as told. A burning sensation shot through her nostrils, up toward her brain, taking her breath away. She'd had her first taste of coke and she hated it. Thomas snorted the rest.

Feeling him kneeling on the bed, he ripped her panties from her behind and rubbed his thumb between the slit of her ass, focusing on her rectum.

Morgan whined and cried. "Oh, my God, please help. Sweet Jesus, please!"

His muscular arm rose in the air once more, before bashing down the back of her head. "Keep quiet, I can't concentrate. You have a pretty ass." He leaned down and inhaled. "Smells good too; you cleaned this ass before leaving the house. You knew you were going to get fucked. You wanted it, slut!" He raised her ass up. "I'm going to give the slut just want she needs." Again, he gathered a mound of phlegm in his throat and spat it between her cheeks, in preparation for the violation soon to come.

She cringed at the thought of her virgin rectum being penetrated.

His thumb wiggled around her crack and then penetrated the hole.

Morgan squealed and her ass became his target.

He took her squealing as his cue to pull her ass into his abdomen. Rubbing against her hole, teasing it, eventually her tight skin gave way to his massive tool. He was inside her, stroking fiercely, and tearing her rectum, as well as her sanity. Morgan cried at the top of her lungs, balling the sheets into her fist, holding on for dear life. She felt skewered. She was the meat and his dick was the stick, piercing her flesh. She felt a warm throb deep inside her stomach. The words *help me* formed in her mouth, but were stuck, she unable to speak.

Tossing her arm behind her back, she tried to push him away from her. He grabbed her arm and pulled up toward her neck. She screamed with excruciating pain. He drilled deeper into her, dismantling her insides, his stick lacerating whatever internal walls her body still supported. As his rhythm increased, so did the pounding of his fist in her back.

Morgan gave up, relaxed herself and thought of being anywhere else, but there. She thought of Franklin. If she wanted to see her baby again, she had to do as the maniac told her.

"You like this, don't you, slut?

She whimpered.

"Yeah, bitch, take this dick all up in that pretty, tight ass." His words blended into a moan, a yell, a kind of cough. She felt hot and gooey spurts shooting deep inside her, shots of wet heat, uninvited venom aimed for the pit of her stomach. She thought she was going to throw up, so she kept her mouth closed tight.

He grunted deeply and hard, as he pulled his penis from her torn rectum. With his thick arm, he reached out for her, grabbing her by the arm, tossing her over onto her back. Her face glistened with tears, snot and saliva.

"Sit up and clean off my dick, slut."

Doing as she was told, she slowly sat up and leaned in close to his penis.

He bald his fist and aimed it at her cheek. "I will break your fucking jaw if you don't move a little faster."

Flinching, fear danced in her eyes. Closing her mouth around the weapon formed against her, he briskly fucked her mouth. Her honey-colored cheeks turned crimson. Instantly, flashes of Lorena clouded her mind. Anger stormed through her and she became crazed. She balled her fist tightly, took him deep down her throat, her lips touching the base of his penis. She held back the desire to regurgitate and looked up at his face. She wanted to see the pain he was about to endure, just as he saw hers. Biting down on his penis as hard she could, she boxed his testicles several times. He hunched over her, hollering to the top of his lungs, harder and stronger than a wounded animal, as she continued Tyson punching him in the nuts. When her top row of teeth met with her bottom row, she released her deadly grasp and hauled off down the hallway. At top speed, she snatched her purse from the sofa and stormed out the house, down the street into the darkness, her jeans newly designed in the back and blood dripping from her fangs.

Running as fast as she could, Morgan stumbled and fell to the ground, landing on a bed of rubble. She looked over her shoulder and focused her eyes sharply, looking for a figure running behind her. Taking a sigh of relief, she sat her exposed behind on the cold gravel and dug deep into her purse, in search of her cell phone. There was only one person she could call. The one person who she knew loved her, regardless.

As she was about to dial the number, she was startled by headlights coming at her at what seemed like top speed. *It was him*, she thought, as fear pierced her heart like a rusty dagger. Jumping backward, she stumbled down into the ditch. Hunching down, she prayed she wouldn't be seen. As the car passed, she released a sigh of relief, she felt safe again. After she pressed send, she placed the small handset to her ear and prayed for an answer.

"I need you," she whimpered into the cell phone. *"Please, help me."*

Chapter 22

It was time to confront Jay, and Cassie was on pins and needles. Knowing he wouldn't be accepting of her decision, she took the necessary precautions by strategically placing utensils throughout her apartment. She didn't own a gun, so she used the next best thing, at least in her mind, knives and forks. All too familiar with Jay's temper, she was going to be prepared should he snap and believe himself to be the next heavyweight champion.

The familiar knock startled her. Looking around, she ensured everything was in place. She took in a deep breath and mumbled, "Stand your ground, girl," as she headed toward the door. "Who is it?" she asked, her hand tightly affixed to the doorknob. Her knees felt weak, as a knot formed in the pit of her stomach. Was she having second thoughts?

"You know who it is, open the damn door."

As the door opened, Jay slowly walked in and looked around, as Cassie stood behind the opened door. "Have a seat," she said, speaking softly.

"What's up?" he asked, with a slight head nod.

Nervously, she remained behind the door until he took a seat on the sofa, closest to the window, yet far enough away from her. Easy listening from WASH 97.1 FM swelled the room.

"Care for a drink?" she offered, hoping his visit would be brief.

"Why do you listen to this shit? Yeah, I'll have a drink."

"It's relaxing," she said, disappearing into the kitchen to fix the drinks, Apple Martini's. Returning with an oval tray set with martini glasses, and a cocktail shaker, she placed the tray on the table and stood erect for a minute, stretching her back, before bartending the drinks. Pouring the apple-flavored intoxicant from the ice-cold silver cocktail shaker, Cassie noticed Jay slightly turning up his nose. "What's wrong?"

"I thought you were fixing me a drink," he said, sarcastically. He wasn't much into the fruity girlie drinks, but if that was all she had to offer, then so be it. He'd get him something stronger later.

Raising her glass, she toasted. "This is all I have in the house. Cheers."

Jay rolled his eyes at her off-handed smart-ass comment and gulped down the drink. "Weak shit."

Cassie shook her head and sat down beside him, making sure she was in arms reach of the knife she cautiously placed under the sofa cushion.

"Jay, we need to talk."

"So talk."

Sipping her drink, she placed it on the cocktail table. Her nervousness was evident.

He leaned forward, resting his arms on his knees, clasping his hands, and intertwining his fingers. "Let me find out your ass is chickening out on me."

"I've come to–"

"Come to what?"

"Listen, Jay, I just don't want any part of it, that's all."

"That bitch killed Marcy!"

Shaking her head in disagreement, she stood and began pacing the floor. "No, no, she did not kill Marcy. All this time, I thought the same thing, but–"

"But what?" he growled, jumping to his feet. "Had Raven not humiliated Marcy the way she did, trying to get back at me because I didn't want to marry her trifling ass, Marcy would be alive."

Fearing the enraged look in his eyes, Cassie stepped away from him, and walked toward the front door. "I think you should leave, Jay. My mind is made up."

"Oh, you think I should leave," he mimicked. "Your mind is made up, huh?" Approaching her, with flared nostrils, Jay pressed his finger deep against her chest. "I will tell you when you've made up your mind."

The warmth of his breath warmed her face. Turning her head to the side, she closed her eyes. She was in trouble, she could feel it in her bones, and she was nowhere near any of the weapons she strategically placed about her apartment. Once her heart jumped up in her throat, forming words seemed impossible. Inside, she screamed for help.

Pressing himself against her, plastering her back against the door, Jay removed his belt and wrapped it around her neck. Cassie remained silent, eyeing him down. Whatever fear she felt, seemed to dissipate as the idea of possibly losing her life, turned to pure anger.

"Don't be no fool, Jay," she whispered between clenched teeth, her head braced firmly against the door. "Killing me won't bring Marcy back and it won't solve a thing."

Wickedly grinning, he forms a noose with his belt. Sweetly pulling her hair free, he powerfully slapped her across the face. She fell to the floor, the end of the belt strap firmly clutched in his hand. Yanking her by the neck, she coughed and gagged, as he dragged her crawling behind him as if he were walking a dog. Walking her into the kitchen, she slid across the linoleum tile floor, ending at the stove. He lifted her up onto the spotless marble counter, facing him. Pulling the belt a little tighter around her neck, he eyed the box of plastic wrap. Reaching over, stretching for the box of plastic wrap, he released the belt.

"Move and I'll fucking kill ya," he snarled, exposing yellow teeth, behind thick blackened lips, from years of smoking too much weed.

Tightly wrapping her with the plastic wrap, he started from her torso and worked up to her breasts; wrapping and rewrapping until she was mummified in Saran Wrap. Using his teeth to tear the sheet of plastic wrap, he licked the ends and sealed her in tight and snug as bug in a rug. Cutting off a long sheet of wrap, two arms length wide, he wrapped it around her face. Unzipping her slacks, he leaned her over to one side and slid her pants down around her butt. Repeating the same steps on the other side, he tugged at her pants until he pulled them off and tossed them across the kitchen floor. Moving in close to her, he leaned in, smiled, and covered her mouth, sucking as much of her breath from her as possible, before moving up to her nose. Sensing her asphyxia, he lowered himself down to her knees, pressed his palms flat against them, and slowly opened her legs. "You're nasty, where are your draws, girl?"

Trained as a professional swimmer, Cassie held in her breath and prayed for a way out. Looking down at him, she focused on her knees.

Catching her eye contact, he said, "Don't even think about it."

Spreading her legs farther apart, he raised the small mound of flesh over her clitoris and stroked beneath it with his finger.

She flinched.

Moving in, he sucked, bit and stroked her clitoris until she quickly came, his face glistened with her nectar. Rising up, he poked a hole in the plastic, beneath her nose. Inserting his finger inside her crotch, he spooned out a sampling of her sex and shoved it up her nose.

"Now, you listen to me, and you listen to me carefully. You *will* do your part. Do I make myself clear?"

Panting, Cassie slowly nodded her head in agreement.

"Good. You're lucky I let you live. Since you're so smart, figure out how you're going to—" he paused and looked at her. Almost on cue, he laughed hysterically. "You look like Queen Nefertiti, all wrapped up and shit."

Tears streamed down her face, adhering to the plastic, her body hot and suffocating.

"Lata," he said, closing the door behind him.

Panic stricken, Cassie looked around for a way to unravel her cocoon. Within minutes, Jay returned.

"Now you didn't think I would really leave you like this, did you?" Tearing the plastic from her face, she slumped over and gagged for air.

"Use your teeth to remove the rest," he laughed, walking toward the door. "I'll call you later with the specifics."

Chapter 23

"You're finished. I'm cutting you off," Terri said, firmly.

A drunken Arthur swiveled his head in her direction. His eyes were bloodshot marbles. Their color reminded her of red wine.

"Who the fuck is you?" Arthur slurred, saliva splattering over the table.

Chas quickly covered his drink.

"I'm the owner," she lied, "you've seen me enough to know. It's my place. It's closing time, no more last call for you."

"I won't come back to this fucking place anymore," he yelled, slamming an empty glass down on the table. "Hey," he paused, trying to focus his eyes, zeroing in as close as he could on Terri's face. "You are *not* the fucking manager. I know him personally and I'm going to have your ass fired for lying," he blurted, with a thick and heavy tongue. Barely making any sense, he continued with, "You wanna fuck me, 'cause Mo won't?"

"Uh, okay, it's time to go," Chas interrupted. Cracking an embarrassing smile at Terri, Chas moved Arthur's glass to the other side of the table, out of his reach. "Sorry about that, Terri."

Terri smiled and began removing the glasses from the table. "Don't worry about it. How about a cup of coffee for your friend?"

Chas nodded in agreement. "Thanks."

Lowering his head, Arthur faced Chas. "What she want with that motherfucker, man?" As tears welled in his eyes, he gently shook his head in denial. "Doesn't she know I love her, Chas?"

Chas sat quietly, not willing to interrupt him. He knew, more than anyone that a man needed to vent. Therefore, regardless of what went down between Arthur and Raven, he was still Arthur's friend and he was going to be there for him, all ears with an open heart.

"She made me do it, Chas. I mean, you know how Raven can be. She said she would tell Morgan about Reneé and I didn't want that. So, I gave in and it was awful. It was like she had her hands up my ass, like a damn puppet, doing everything on her command." His face became a glowering mask of rage, furious at his vulnerability to Raven. His lips thinned with anger, as he spewed his contempt for Raven. "I could kill that bitch!"

Chapter 24

It was a flat, moonless night, not another car in sight and Raven turned on the high beams. Lottsford Road was so dark it felt as if black curtains were hanging over the night sky. A raccoon darted across the road in front of Raven's Mustang GT, causing her to slam on the brakes. Quickly glancing in the rearview mirror, Raven closed her eyes for a second before continuing down the narrow, two-lane road. Slowly releasing the clutch, she peered out the window toward the ditch. Something bulky, like a huge bag of trash lay still. Coming to a complete stop, she rolled down the passenger window and called out. "Mo, is that you?"

"Ray," Morgan cried hysterically, pulling herself to her feet.

"Oh my God!" Raven backed up down the road, slapped the gear in first, and quickly pulled over to the side of the road. The high beams were a spotlight for Morgan. Tears blinded her eyes and choked her voice as Morgan stood before her helpless and in pain. Jumping out of the car, Raven sprinted toward Morgan and embraced her. "Who did this to you? What happened?"

Burying her face in Raven's neck, Morgan wept aloud, as Raven rocked her from side to side. Gulping hard, hot tears flowed down her cheeks. "I can't go home."

"Did Arthur do this to you? If he did, I will kill his ass—"

Shaking her head profusely, "No, no, it wasn't Arthur. He would never do anything to harm me. He," she paused, because at that moment, it finally dawned on her. She silently wept inside before speaking. "He loves me too much." She glared at Raven and suppressed the mental images of her husband giving his passionate love to her sister.

Leading her toward the car, every fiber in Raven's body seethed with rage. *Whoever did this to you, Morgan, will pay, and pay dearly.* "That motherfucker ain't gettin' away with this shit!"

Easing into the passenger seat, Morgan sat motionless, staring in front of her.

With cool authority, Raven said, "He must live some where around here."

Morgan never uttered a word. She had every intention of dealing with Thomas, but now wasn't the time. The last thing she wanted was Raven going off half hazard. When she spoke, her voice was tender, almost a murmur. "He'll pay."

Biting her lip, Raven looked at Morgan. Recognizing the cold look in Morgan's eyes, Raven hadn't seen this side of Morgan in years, since the *untimely* passing of their aunt, who became their guardian after their parent's death. "I'm down with whatever, sis," Raven assured her. "But, for now, I'm taking you to the hospital."

The emergency room at the Doctor's Hospital was nearly empty and it wasn't long before a nurse was able to see Morgan. While she was being seen, Raven glanced through the tattered magazines in the waiting room.

Three hours later, Morgan appeared, being escorted by a man in a white coat. Raven stood up and looked at her watch. It was 3:37 a.m. Morgan nodded to the doctor and walked toward her. Raven tried to guess from her expression what was going on, but Morgan wasn't smiling.

"Mo, everything okay?"

Morgan smiled faintly. "No, but I'll be fine."

"Well, what did they say?"

"Who are they, Ray?" Morgan snapped, becoming annoyed with herself for calling Thomas in the first place. "I had to have stitches in my ass, okay? I took an AIDS test too."

Raven wrapped her arms tightly around her sister, and kissed her on the cheek. "What did he do to you," she cried.

Sniffling, Morgan, embraced her sister tighter and buried her face in her neck. "He raped me. He did things to me that," she paused. Loosening the embrace, Morgan looked into Raven's eyes. "Ray, I guess we're all even. Arthur cheated on me with you and I cheated on him with a rapist."

148

Swiping her thumb across Morgan's cheek, Raven closed her eyes, drew in a deep breath and looked, honestly, at Morgan. "We've been through a lot, you know. And, we will get through this." Smiling, Raven kissed her sister's forehead. "Let's go home."

"I can't go home," Morgan hesitated.

"Why not?"

"Arthur saw me tonight, with…him."

"Oh I see."

"Franklin! I have to get my baby."

"Where is he?"

"With Veronica."

"Oh okay, well, we'll call Veronica and ask if she can keep him until tomorrow afternoon, until you can get yourself together. He will be fine with Veronica."

"Come on, let's go." Walking out of the hospital, toward her car, Raven asked, "What's his name again, Mo?"

"Who?"

"The rapist."

"Thomas."

"Does he have a last name?"

"Whittaker," she responded. "Leave some of that ass for me."

The tree-lined street of Princess Garden Parkway appeared peaceful at almost four in the morning. Raven remained silent. There was no way she would tell Morgan, right then, what was really going on with her—pregnant with her sister's niece or nephew and stepchild. But she knew it would have to be soon. Right then, it felt as if all was well and she missed that feeling.

Chapter 25

Arthur remembered the first time he had ever seen Morgan. Angelic and graceful, a beholding sight, he smiled as he thought about the way she walked, like a duck, with the nerve to have a switch in her hips too. Instantly, she became his best friend, his source of inspiration and his desire for her to never want again in life.

How could he have been so weak, copulating with his wife's sister? *Country, hillbillies did that kind of shit, not me,* he thought to himself as he paced the floor, wondering what had happened to his spine. He looked around the big empty house and couldn't imagine it without Morgan and Franklin. Thoughts of Franklin brightened his face as he imagined his father-son talk about sex and girls. The first thing he would tell him is to never marry a woman with a sister.

At that moment, Arthur heard a car pull up in the driveway. Headlights flooded through the window. Walking over to the window, he slightly pulled the curtain to the side. Anger rose from deep within when he saw Raven's Mustang. *I can't believe she has the nerve to show up this time of night!*

Hopping out of the driver's side, Raven ran to the other side of the car and opened the passenger door.

Arthur grimaced; his face looked as if someone had punched him in his stomach when he saw Morgan hobble out of the car. Still in somewhat of a drunken stupor, Arthur swaggered to the front door before Morgan could insert her key.

The door flung open. "What are you doing here," he slurred at Raven, his tongue heavy and thick. Pointing his finger at her, "You are always keeping up trouble," he accused.

"Shut up, Arthur, and get out of the way," Morgan ordered.

Arthur stood erect, a stern look washed over his face. "No, I will not," he said, holding his head up, looking down his nose at Morgan. "You are no better–" Pausing, he pointed at Raven and continued, "No better than that tramp sister of yours!"

"Arthur, take your drunken ass in the fucking house, before you get hurt," Raven suggested, before she kissed Morgan on the cheek. "I'll call you later. Okay?"

"No, fuck you, Raven! Fuck you, fuck you, fuck you, fuck you, fuck you, fuck you, fuck you–"

"Okay, can you please stop?" Morgan pushed Arthur inside the house and closed the door. "You are ridiculous."

"What were you doing with her? She is the enemy!"

Morgan remained calm. She had been through enough and surely was not in the mood to breastfeed Arthur's ass. "She's my sister."

"You mean after all she did to you, you're still gonna be her sister?"

Morgan looked at Arthur, heavily sighed and walked into the kitchen.

Following on her heels, Arthur continued. "Where is my son?"

"He's fine."

"I didn't ask you *how* he was, I asked you where *was* he!"

Morgan sat her purse on the counter, opened the cupboard and pulled down a glass. "He's staying the night with Veronica."

"Oh." Leaning against the wall, Arthur folded his arms across his chest. He intently watched his wife. Something about her was different. She was walking funny and moving too slow. "I saw you tonight."

"Yes, Arthur, I saw you too."

"You fucked him, didn't you?"

Reaching inside the refrigerator for the carton of orange juice, Morgan ignored the question.

"Morgan, I can't believe you cheated on me!"

Facing him, she gave a forced smile. Shaking her head in dismay, Morgan placed the carton of orange juice on the table. "I should throw this glass at your fucking head, you bastard. How dare you? You have a lot of fucking nerve, standing there accusing me of shit you already did, more times than I care to know." Slamming the glass on the table, Morgan walked past Arthur, brushing up against his arm. "You asshole," she mumbled.

Chapter 26

Making love to Chas was one of the most exquisite and disconcerting experiences of her life. Palms flat against each other, forearms following suit and at every point along her body, her flesh and bone pressed against his. Thighs rising up his hips, she took him inside of her as her legs slid down the backs of his, her heels clamping just below his knees and he felt enveloped, as if he had melted through her flesh, and their souls had joined.

She cried out and he could feel it as if it came from his own vocal cords.

"Jo," he whispered as he disappeared inside her, blending with the cream she expelled, just by his touch. "I love you, Mrs. Walker."

Making low moans, she wrapped her legs around his buttocks and pushed him deeper insider. "I love you too, Mr. Walker."

Arching his back, Chas stroked his wife to be with swift passionate strokes, connecting with the soft walls of her vagina, then slightly raising up to stroke the knot at the opening of her cave. Feeling the small bump against his rod, he intensely focused on her eyes as he rhythmically stroked her.

From the look on her face, he knew he was hitting that spot just right. "Is that it, babe?"

Unable to speak, she nodded her head, the prolong anticipation was almost unbearable, needing to explode before his intense stroking sent her into a frenzy.

His strokes quickening, he covered her mouth, stealing the sweetness of her breath.

Digging her nails deep into his back, scraping down to his ass, she squeezed, pushing him in to her. "That's it," she managed to say. "Don't stop fuckin' me." Her cream complexion flushed, her lips parted, her back arched as she whispered, "Don't… stop…fuckin'…me."

The hot intensity he felt between her legs, along with the friction of his throbbing rod inside stroking against her pulsating wall, brought him to a more than satisfying climax he'd never felt before. "Oh shit," he yelled, his face distorting, his strokes becoming rapid, with quick pounding strokes. "Uh, uh, uh, ohhhh."

"Yes! Oh baby, yes, fuck me motherfucker!" Jo yelled at the top of her lungs, as her thighs tightly gripped around his waist, while her muscles contracted against his exploding member.

The Eagles' *Desperado* wafted from the radio, in unison with the annoying buzz of the alarm. Stretching her leg high in the air, Jo yawned and flipped over onto her stomach. "What a song to wake up to," she said, her face muffled in the pillow.

"I love that song," Chas said, swinging his legs off the side of the bed, his toes touching the cold wood flooring. "I like the melody."

"Yeah, the lyrics aren't bad either," Jo chuckled, stroking the lower part of Chas' back. "Good morning, baby. How did you sleep?"

Twisting around and leaning down on his forearm, he kissed Jo on the back of her neck. "Morning, babe. I slept like a baby." Standing, Chas stretched his arms above his head and yawned. "You want coffee?" he asked, walking toward the bathroom.

"Yes, please." When she heard the bathroom door close, she yelled, "What's on your agenda today, babe?"

Opening the bathroom door, Chas turned on the faucet and began washing his hands. "I'm showing a couple of houses today. What about you?"

"I'm leaving work at twelve to meet with the wedding coordinator."

Walking back into the bedroom, Chas opened the door to the walk-in closet and turned on the light. "Wanna go out for dinner tonight?"

"Sounds good." Jo stirred in bed before sitting upright, then leaning back against the headboard. "Sweetie, aren't you the least bit curious about the wedding plans."

"Nope, I trust you."

"Well, that's good to know, but it would be nice to have you planning it with me."

Choosing the chocolate brown suit, with faint pink pinstripes, Chas exited the closet and helped up a tie. "How does this tie go with this suit?"

"Fine. I've always loved that suit on you." Jo folded her arms across her chest in annoyance.

Noticing, Chas dropped the suit to his side and tilted his head. "Honey, you know that's not my thing, which is why you have the coordinator and I'm probably going to be paying out the nose," he chuckled.

"No, you won't pay out the nose. It's going to be quaint, with only family."

"Sounds perfect." He blew her a kiss and headed toward the bathroom to turn on the shower.

"Chas, what about your tux? I haven't seen it yet."

"I know. Don't worry; you'll see it when we're taking our vows."

Jo perked up, shot out of the bed, and darted to the bathroom. "Huh? Hell to the naw, Chas!"

Lathering his face with shaving cream, Chas looked at her through the mirror and chuckled. "You'll love it, trust me."

Shaking her head in defiance, "No, no, no! I will not have my wedding looking jacked up," she barked.

He faced her. "Jo, I haven't seen your wedding dress."

"So?"

157

"So? If I can't see your wedding dress, why do you have to see my wedding suit?"

"Okay, now you're being silly, Chas! I have to make sure we coordinate. And, it's a tuxedo."

"We always coordinate just like we are now. We're both in the nude and we match perfectly, wouldn't you say?"

Rolling her eyes, she turned her back to him and headed back to the bedroom. "You better not look like a hot fucking mess, that's all I'm saying."

He chuckled. "Or what?"

"Or I'm gonna whip that ass!"

Chapter 27

Raven hated throwing up more than anything; hated the taste in her mouth, the burn in her throat, the way she shook afterward. Throwing up in the toilet, nothing inside her but yellow phlegm and dry heaving, she cried, coughed, and cried some more until there wasn't anything left to throw up.

Morning sickness.

Wiping her mouth with the back of her hand, Raven lifted herself off the floor and flushed the toilet, then closed the lid. Turning on the water faucet, she cupped her hands under the stream—sips, swoosh around, spit, sip, swoosh around, spits.

Sitting on the commode, Raven lowered her head between her knees and silently sobbed. She couldn't destroy Morgan again. She had to do something. But what was she going to do? Was she to have an abortion? She didn't believe in taking a life, which is truly any oxymoron, considering how she so mercilessly took the lives of Ramone and Reneé.

Thoughts of that night were as vivid as if it had taken place the night before. A wicked smile crossed her face when she thought about how Ramone acted like a bitch on a street corner, begging to be paid to suck a john's dick.

On that fateful night at The Renaissance in downtown Washington, DC, sweat glistened like oil on Ramone's bruised naked body, as Raven had his wrists and ankles securely tied to the four-poster bed, of the Executive Suite. With an enormous strap-on dildo, Raven drilled into his asshole vigorously and frequently, as Ramone howled from the torturous pain. The chocolate, vibrating mass of rubber had become an extension of her being, and the role of dominatrix had adrenaline pumping through her veins at top speed. She was high off control, the best feeling in the world, and she loved every minute of it. She enjoyed inflicting pain on a man who had pained her with his lies, deceit and betrayal—punishment for her not finding out about him earlier. He had beaten her at her motto, *Do unto you before you do unto me*, and he had to pay. And, boy did he pay, straight through the ass. By the time Raven finished with Ramone, the tiny hole of his rectum was torn and stretched wider than the opening of a tunnel, which is a stretch, no pun intended, but point made.

After hours of inhumane treatment, Raven ordered Ramone to call Reneè, his wife who, unfortunately for her, had pursued Arthur. And, because Raven always had Morgan's best interest at heart, she had to exterminate Arthur's pest as well.

While waiting for Reneè to arrive, Ramone realized that his fate was in Raven's hands, and he probably would never see sunlight again, so he figured he would tell her how he really felt. But first, he would try to talk his way out of his restraints. After all, there was a time when Ramone had so much control over Raven, he had her lying in the doorway of her apartment while he sucked, nibbled, and practically pierced her clitoris, for all to see, including her neighbor. What did he have to lose? Absolutely nothing...well, maybe his life.

"Ray, aren't you going to untie me?" Ramone pleaded, trying to gain her sympathy.

Raven looked over her shoulder at him and smirked. "Do I look like a fucking fool to you?"

"Please, Ray, I'm in so much pain." A true understatement, as his rectum felt like a four-alarm blaze.

"Good!"

"Please, Ray."

She faced him and leaned against the wall with her arms folded across her chest. "Ramone, I don't give a rat's ass if you're in pain."

Ramone had become enraged. "You crazy bitch, I was good to you! Why are you doing this?"

Raven didn't think she liked his attitude; after all, she was giving his rectum a break. How selfish of him! Casually strolling over to the satchel bag situated on the floor, next to the nightstand, Raven knelt down and reached inside the satchel, where she retrieved the .22-caliber from its holster.

Ramone's eyes widened and flooded with fear and tears.

She squatted down before him. "Ramone, did you really think you could get away with lying to me?"

"Oh God, please don't kill me," he cried. "I was wrong for not telling you about Reneè, but I didn't think it would've made a difference. You said you only wanted the dick and nothing more," he sobbed and whimpered.

"Ramone, you hurt me. I gave myself to you for three years. You did things to me I would've never allowed anyone to do to me. You brought another man into my home to fuck me while you watched."

"But I thought it was what you wanted?"

"Yes, and thanks to you, I'm with Chas now."

"Fuck Chas!" he yelled at the top of his lungs, with more venom than a poisonous snake. For Ramone, the gloves were off. Well, not figuratively, because he was tied, face down, to the bed.

She waved her index finger in his face, in a 'shame-on-you' fashion. "Ooh, that's not very nice of you, Ramone."

"Man, why did he have to go and tap my pussy?"

"You're the one who led the horse to the water. He simply took a drink."

"He will never be me," he snarled, his body heaving as he is now enraged with anger.

"You're right once again. Chas will never be like you because he has what you don't."

"Yeah, and what's that?"

"Me." She smiled as her eyes roamed his body, finally meeting his glare without flinching.

Raven loved sexing Ramone more than eating. He did things to her that made her lose her mind. However, he had to mess it up by not telling her he was married. As far as she was concerned, Ramone was no different from Jay, the no-good bastard who jilted her at the altar.

"Bitch, you are old news. Yeah, I had my way with you. I fucked you when and where I wanted. You're the dumb bitch for allowing me to do it to your ass."

Raven's brow raised in anger. "I suggest you shut the fuck up," she spoke between clinched teeth. His words had gotten her hotter than hell and given her an itchy trigger finger.

He ignored her words of caution and continued taunting her. "Yeah, I did what the fuck I wanted to do to you," he cackled. "Remember the time you got on your knees and sucked my dick in a pissy ass alley in Anacostia?"

Raven grimaced at the thought. She remembered all too well. It was during a time when she ate, slept, and shitted Ramone. Everything he asked of her, she accommodated.

"Uh huh, and since we're going back down memory lane," he continued prodding at her. "Remember the time I took you over to my boy's crib and the fellas ran a train on your freak nasty ass?" His laughter was uncontrollable, reminiscent of the Joker from Batman & Robin.

She slowly stood up. Her chest heaved with each deep breath she took. She felt her pressure rising. Beads of perspiration danced on her forehead. "Yes, I remember," she whispered as she hovered over him. She forced a smile. "Those were the good old days."

"I fucked your ass royally and you loved it. The only difference between you and those tricks on 14th and U Streets is you do it for free, you dumb bitch!" He gathered a wad of phlegm in his mouth and spat it in her face, leaving her with the burning desire to end his life. "Chas can have your used up ass. Your shit's been stretched so wide, it's like the fucking black hole. Besides, no man wants to feel like he's putting his dick out a window, you loose bitch." Still laughing hysterically in her face, "You used to be tight. Now my dick gets lost up in ya," he hollered with laughter to the top of his lungs. He lowered his head and raised his brow. His eyeballs rolled up toward the ceiling, almost rolling to the back of his head, showing only the whites of his eyes. "You better kill me, girl," he snarled. "'Cause if you let me loose, I will kill you for sure."

Ramone's words stung deep and the blood running through her veins was at its boiling point. Her hands shook and her knees weakened. She felt like she was on shaky ground. She felt queasy and her breathing turned into short pants. Nevertheless, she maintained her cool, despite the cheap, demeaning comments.

"Anything else you need to get off your chest, baby?" she asked, reaching for the pillow lying next to his bruised head.

164

With uncontrollable laughter, barely getting his words out, he said, "Yeah, does Arthur know you and Morgan be swapping pussy juices? If you can get nasty with that Marcy chick, I know you wouldn't have a problem doing your sister." Ramone went for the jugular and attacked the one person in her life who meant the world to her, demeaning Morgan in one breath. There was no way in hell she was going to let him get away with it. She ignored the Marcy comment. She knew he had probably heard it from Chas.

Raven held the pillow close to her chest and Ramone knew his fate as he pleaded to have his life spared. "Look, man, don't do this. I have two kids, Raven. They can't be without their daddy."

Raven tilted her head back and released a deep sigh. "They were without their daddy every night you spent in my bed."

"Please don't do this!" he hollered as loud as he could, in hopes that someone would hear him. "Oh God, please, Raven!! HELP!! Oh God, I am so sorry. I was wrong. I promise I won't do anything to you and I will leave you be, if you'll let me live, please. I'm begging you, Ray!" Panic like the one he'd never known welled in his throat, causing him to choke.

Raven was unnerved by Ramone's plead for his life. She placed the pillow over his head, smothering his cries. She wrapped her hands around the gun and lowered it into the pillow, pressing it against the back of his head. She bit down hard on her lower lip and closed her eyes.

BANG!

Ramone's body jolted and then went limp from the muffled gunshot to the back of the head. Blood splattered against the headboard. The white cotton sheets became the canvas for Raven's handiwork, a collage of red spots, streaks, and brain matter.

"Look at what you made me do," she said to the bloodstained pillow. Her voice was emotionless. "I told you to stop running your mouth."

In the blink of an eye, Ramone was face-to-face with his maker.

Raven cleaned that room better than The Cleaner in *Pulp Fiction*. As she gathered her things and proceeded toward the door, a knock stopped her in her tracks.

"Damn, who the fuck is it?" she mouthed. She had forgotten about Reneè.

She contemplated whether she should respond to the knock. She desperately wanted to vacate the room. Being so close to Ramone's dead body was a little too close for her comfort.

The knock was persistent.

"Ramone, it's me, Reneè. Open the door."

Raven slowly tiptoed to the door and looked through the peephole. She swallowed hard and squared her shoulders. The door opened slowly and Reneè stood frozen in the doorway.

"Ramone!" she called out as she put one foot in front of the other and slowly walked through the door, almost as if her feet were pulling several pounds of concrete. She was about to speak as the sight of her husband's dead, badly bruised body stopped her in her tracks. She wrapped her arms tightly around her and cried out like a wounded animal, "Oh my God!" She stood motionless in the middle of the room. Although the pillow was over her husband's head, she knew his lean, muscular body quite well. Thoughts ran rampant through her mind. She didn't know what to do. She was afraid to move. The door slammed and startled her.

Raven stood face-to-face before her enemy. "Hello Reneè." She walked toward the bed. "Well, you finally made it. You almost missed me."

Reneè took her stare off Ramone's corpse and directed it toward Raven. "Did you do this?"

"Naw, he did it to himself." She dropped her hands to her side. "He was a bad boy and he had to be punished." She shrugged her shoulders. "Discipline is a bitch."

Reneè stood in shock. Her eyes moved from Raven, to the door, to the phone. She looked confused.

"If I were you, I would think twice about reaching for the phone or the door. I'm pretty much shit intolerant, as you can see." Raven pointed at Ramone's corpse.

Reneè slowly walked over to the bed and knelt down beside her husband. "But why? I don't understand."

"Sure you do. You understand fully. From what I hear, you know all about me."

A puzzled look flashed across Reneè's face. "Are you Raven?"

"Who else would it be?"

"I can't believe you did this."

"Listen, the way I see it, you have three choices. One, I can keep you alive and spend the rest of my life behind bars for killing your two-timing husband, and that isn't going to happen." Raven pulled the .22-caliber from the satchel and walked around the bed to where Reneè stood. "Two, I can have you lie face down beside him, place a pillow over your head, and you two can spend the rest of eternity in hell." She picked up a pillow. "Or three, I can have you lie face up on the bed, place the pillow over your face and shoot you in the head, then place the gun in your hand and call it a murder suicide."

"You have it all planned out, huh?" Reneè stuttered, wringing her hands together. "You will never get away with this."

"Yada, yada, yada…what will it be—one, two, or three?"

"I prefer four," Reneè shouted as she jumped to her feet and kicked her right leg toward Raven's face, attempting to knock the gun from her hand. Unfortunately, she slipped up, knocked her head against the corner of the oak-carved nightstand and fell unconscious.

Raven looked down at Reneè with a questionable look. "Now why would you go and do some dumb shit like that?" Raven grabbed Reneè by her weave and lifted her to the bed, lying her face up beside her beloved Ramone. She wrinkled up her nose at the smell of intercourse around Reneè's mouth. She placed the pillow over her face. "Enjoy hell, bitch," she snarled as she pulled the trigger, firing a muffled gunshot to the side of Reneè's head.

The numbness of her ass from the toilet seat snapped her back to reality. Smiling, she thought of the natural high that came from doing all of the bullshit she had done in the past, to people who were deserving of her backlash. However, though, as her smile turned upside down, Morgan didn't deserve any of what she received. Raven was determined to make things better between her and Morgan. She missed the midday lunch and shopping sprees they used to take, and how Morgan made her laugh, way down, belly-deep. There was no excuse for her indiscretion, if you could call it that, and she planned to make it up to Morgan and she knew exactly what she was going to do.

Moving from the bathroom to the small nook in the corner of the living room she used as her home office, Raven turned on her computer, entwined her fingers, cracked her knuckles and got down to business. Using her trusty ZabaSearch.com, she typed in "Thomas Whittaker" in the state of "Maryland" and sat back, awaiting the results. Fucking with her sister, he didn't know what being fucked in the ass truly felt like until he'd been fucked in the ass by her. And, she planned to fuck him royally, in many ways.

"Ah, Mr. Thomas Whittaker. Surprise, surprise, surprise," she said, with a wicked smile on her face. Using the address given by ZabaSearch.com, she pulled up the directions from her place to his, on MapQuest.com, to make sure the address given was in the same vicinity where she picked up Morgan on Lottsford Road. If it was, she knew she had her man. "I've got your ass now, you fucking rapist!"

Calling the police was not an option for Raven. Jail would have been too good for Thomas Whittaker. No, he was about to spend time in Raven's jail, which, for him, will be the equivalent of spending eternity in hell. She was planning to set that ass on fire, literally. Probably figuratively, if the mood strikes her.

As she mentally develops her retaliation plan on Mr. Whittaker, the phone rings. It's Cassie.

"We need to talk," Cassie said, before Raven could utter a word.

"Hello to you too."

"Are you home?"

"Duh, where did you call me? Why are you sounding so crazy?"

"I'm on my way over." Cassie hung up before she could respond.

Raising a brow, "Okay," Raven said, returning back to her thoughts. She was seeking vengeance on behalf of her sister, and woe unto Mr. Whittaker.

From ZabaSearch.com, she was able to retrieve his phone number. For her plan to work, he needed to be home. And, two days before Christmas, she was sure he'd be home, if he wasn't traveling to visit family. For his sake, he would want to be visiting family.

Chapter 28

Chas leaned back in his chair and propped his feet on top of the desk at Walker Realty. The love of his life soaked his thoughts with pleasure. He was so in love with Jo. Everything about her, and them, felt right, which is why he knew he had made the right decision when he asked her to marry him. Jo had a way of making him feel like a man, allowing him to take the lead, in and out of bed, and in public.

The smile in his eyes contained a sensuous flame when he thought back to that cool February, a year ago, when he met Jo. He thought Raven was the boldest woman he'd ever met, but Jo took the cake, as well as his breath. He thought she was the most beautiful woman he'd seen, with heart-shaped pouting lips and a smooth cream complexion. Her curvaceous hips and small waistline reminded him of Jessica Rabbit. At that time, he was getting over his short relationship with Raven. Had he known then about Raven, what he knew now, he wouldn't have touched that lunatic with someone else's dick.

He enjoyed reminiscing about Jo. He loved the way she tilted her head to one side, stealing a look at him. She didn't think he saw it, but he did. He saw and, committed to memory, every word, every move she made, and the way she smelled, like sandalwood. Was it possible to have spotted his soul mate, a few feet from him, without truly knowing her soul? He didn't know, but he was determined to find out. Little did Jo know; Chas was on her from the time she walked through the door.

Chas sat at the bar, as Jo made her way toward him. Approaching him, she frantically searched for the right words, for she was not accustomed to approaching men; they always approached her. His attire was simple, but rich. Standing behind him, she inhaled deeply and wrapped herself in his masculine scent. Devastatingly handsome, she couldn't take her eyes off him. He was making her hot and she was finding it hard to control the urge to jump his bones, but of course, she was a woman on a hunt, determined to snag her prey.

She softly cleared her throat and tapped him on the shoulder. "Hello."

He faced her with his fingers wrapped tightly around his snifter of Cognac. "Hi," he responded, smiling widely.

"May I have a moment of your time?" she nervously stumbled, her ecru cheeks turning terracotta.

He smiled and extended his hand toward her. "I'm Chas. Would you like a drink?"

"I'm Jo, and a drink would be nice. Thank you."

Chas motioned for the bartender. "Whatever the lady is drinking."

"Cranberry and vodka," Jo ordered, then glanced over her shoulder and smiled at the peanut gallery that kept watch of her every move.

Chas offered Jo his seat and stood close behind her. "So what do I owe the pleasure?"

"Well, umm…"

"Cat got your tongue?" he chuckled.

"No, not at all. I find you very attractive and would like to get to know you."

Chas released an irresistible grin. "You would, huh?"

Jo thought how his dimples reminded her of deep caves. She was tempted to stick her finger inside his cave, but she thought she was already being too forward as it was, and she wasn't going to lead him to believe this was a regular routine with her.

"Will that be a problem?"

His smile widened with his approval. "No problem at all."

"So, Chas, are you single, married, divorced, involved, or widowed?"

"Single. And you?"

"Single, but looking," she replied in a low, sultry voice.

Chas stared at Jo and then burst out laughing. His laughter was deep, warm, and rich.

Jo laughed gently. "What's so funny?" she asked.

"That 'single, but looking' comment was funny. If you're single, of course you're looking," he said.

"Not necessarily. You could be single and not looking for shit."

Chas chuckled, took a sip of his drink, and smiled. "My bad." The smile in his eyes contained a sensuous flame.

Jo smiled and moved in closer. "Could we exchange numbers?"

Chas tilted his head back in thought and pouted his full lips. "Yeah, I'd like that."

After asking the bartender for a pen, she wrote her phone number down on a crumpled white napkin, folded it neatly, and placed it securely in Chas' hand. She leaned in closer and whispered, "Don't wait too long to call me."

He cupped her chin tenderly in his warm hand and pulled her close to him. His breath penetrated her nostrils, leaving her with wet panties. His lips curled into a smile. "Stay by the phone," he whispered as his lips brushed against hers with a feathery swipe.

With weak legs, wet panties, and a shortness of breath, Jo walked through the crowd while trying to maintain her composure.

However, it didn't stop there. Chas smiled, nodded, and downed the remainder of his drink. As Jo sashayed through the doors and into the night, he reached in his pocket and pulled out his cell phone. He unfolded the crumpled napkin she had given him, and smiled as he dialed the telephone number. When she answered, he said, "Your wish is my command," in a deep monotone voice that gave her chills from the top of her head to the tips of her chubby toes.

"So I see. Keep this up and I'll have to give you a treat for being obedient."

"Well then, I'll continue to be good. I want my treat."

Chas hung up the phone and Jo screamed to the top of her lungs.

Shaking his head, he couldn't wait to marry Jo. He thought he was in love with Raven, but when he met Jo, he realized he was more in lust with Raven than anything else. Amazed at Raven being so uninhibited, turned Chas on. There was nothing he wouldn't do for her, because she was his woman. Period. However, though, after the call he received from Arthur, after Marcy's suicide, there was something about Raven he found disturbing.

"Chas, its Arthur. Do you think you can meet me at Raven's place? I'm on my way over there now. I will wait for you in the parking lot. This whole thing is not sitting easy with me and I would prefer some back up, if you know what I mean."

"Yeah, no problem. Hey man, I think I know what's going on," Chas said, pacing the floor with a tight grip on the receiver.

"Yeah, what is it?"

"Arthur, man, I just heard on the news about a woman that was found dead in her apartment Sunday morning. The police are calling it an apparent suicide."

"Chas, I'm not following you. What does that have to do with us?"

"Arthur, the dead woman's name is Marcy Douglas."

"Okay, do you know her or something?"

"Man, I don't know. I mean, there was a chick that Raven was hanging out with all day Saturday. Man, her name is Marcy!"

"Oh my God. Do you think...?"

"Man, I don't know what to think. I hope like hell that there is no connection, for Ray's sake. Listen, I'm on my way out the door and I'll be there in fifteen minutes," Chas said, hanging up the phone, grabbing his car keys and closing the door behind him.

Chas shook off the chilly thought of Raven having anything to do with Marcy's death. After all, it was a suicide. But, then again, what about Ramone and Reneé? Again, Chas shook off the thought and moved on to sweeter dreams of Jo.

Checking his watch, Chas decided to call it a day and begins to clear the client files from his desk and neatly tuck them away in his bottom desk file drawer. As he grabs his briefcase, the phone rings. It's Jo.

"How's your day going, handsome?"

"If you're asking if I was able to get any work done, the answer is no."

"No? What have you been doing all day then?"

"Thinking about you."

"Alright now, don't mess around and end up getting a treat before dinner."

Chas chuckled. "What do you want, woman?"

"Nothing, just calling to say hey."

"Hey!"

"You know, I was thinking, babe–"

"Ut oh, that could be dangerous."

"Shut up!"

Chas rolled over with laughter. He wished he were standing before her; he loved to see her cheeks turn blush pink when he slightly annoys her. "Go ahead, babe."

"Anyway, as I was about to say, I don't think we should have a wedding."

Chas felt an instant squeeze of hurt, momentarily breaking his heart. "What do you mean? You don't want to marry me?" His voice broke miserably.

Her slight chuckle was music to his ears, pumping the brakes on the panic that shot through him. "Don't be silly, honey. I love you. You're stuck with me for the rest of your life."

"Whew, you scared me for a minute."

"I didn't say I didn't want to marry you. I *said* I don't think we should have a *wedding*."

"Why not?"

"I want something more intimate, with just you and me."

"Hmm, the Justice of the Peace."

"Well, not so informal, but close."

Chas leaned back in his chair and, once again, propped his feet up on the desk. He loosened the tie around his neck. "Tell me what you have in mind, my love."

"Okay. You, me, a preacher man, and waves crashing against white sand beaches—"

"I love the sound of that, babe. Are you thinking the Bahamas?"

"Yes! I've already checked with a travel agent that can help us find the perfect place that does those kinds of things. You know, perform weddings and stuff. And, we can honeymoon there too."

"I think it's a great idea, babe. And, I think we should celebrate," he said, caressing his swelling crotch, "just as soon as I get home."

"You better bring that ass on, 'cause a sistah is already home, undressed, and fingering herself!" They both laughed.

"See you soon. I love you, Jo."

"I love you too, baby."

Chapter 29

When Cassie finally arrived at Raven's, she was a bundle of nerves. She walked in the door pacing. Stopping, a flicker of apprehension coursed through her. She stared at Raven and then down at the floor, then back at Raven.

"What in the hell is wrong with you?"

Cassie gasped, her body stiffened. "I don't quite know how to say it," she said, wringing her hands together.

"Sit down and say it. All that pacing makes me nervous." Raven headed toward the kitchen. She returned carrying two shot glasses, with a bottle of Patron tucked under her arm. "You look like you need a drink. Damn, you act like you've seen ghosts or some shit." Filling the shot glasses beyond the rim, Patron splattering onto the table, Raven slowly extended the shot glass toward Cassie, careful not to spill any on the carpet. "Take it to the head, girl. You're scaring me."

Taking the shot glass, Cassie closed her eyes, raised the glass until it brushed against her lips and consumed the firewater, allowing the liquid heat to flow down the back of her throat.

"Wooooooooweee!" she squealed, slamming the glass on the table. "Damn!"

Raven fell out with laughter. "I take it you've never had Patron before."

"That shit is strong; will put hair on your chest!"

"Okay, what's on your mind, Cass?"

Leaning back on the sofa, Cassie decided to broach the topic the best way she knew how, straight to the point. "Jay is seeking revenge on you. He is planning to fuck you up really bad, Raven."

Panic, as Raven had never known, welled in her throat, as sheer fright swept through her. For the first time, someone else was seeking revenge on her. However, she sat quietly, listening, determined not to reveal to Cassie how she felt. She refused to let Cassie see her sweat, or anyone else for that matter.

"It's payback for Marcy," Cassie continued. "He said you killed her and you deserve to be judged by a jury of your peers, which–"

"And, he's my jury, huh?"

Cassie nodded.

"Why are you telling me all of this?"

"Because," she paused. "In the beginning I was in on the plan too. But, after spending time with you, I didn't want to have any parts of the plan."

"Oh, I see," Raven replied, trying not to sound frightened. But, she was finding it hard to do. She really was afraid of Jay. She knew him too well, and he, if anyone else, was time enough for her. She remembered when she ran into him in the elevator at work.

She was leaving for the day when she bumped into him in the elevator. It was quite awkward, working in the same building, and, on occasion, bumping into the man who abandoned her at the altar. Jay and Raven's encounter wasn't pleasant for her. Roles were swapped that day, and when she sought revenge, she went after the weakest link, Marcy, who was, at that time, Jay's current girlfriend.

"So Jay, how are you doing?" she said, when she stepped onto the elevator, standing on the opposite side.

"I'm doing fine, thanks. I can't complain."

Her defenses were weakened when she got a whiff of his cologne, causing her to blurt out, "I've missed you."

"I've missed you too, Ray. I must admit, seeing you do bring back old memories."

At the moment, she felt she had him in her web. "Well, let's do something about it," she said, as she stepped toward him.

"What are you talking about?" She pressed the stop button on the elevator panel. "Ray, what are you doing?"

She dropped her belongings to the floor, "Making up for lost time, baby," she said as she loosened his tie, before she softly kissed his lips.

"Raven, we can't do this. This is not appropriate."

Ignoring his bullshit plea, because she knew better, she pressed up against hardening manhood, grinding it against her pelvic bone. "Why Jay, are you committed?" she asked him, like she really cared. She was a woman on a mission and intended to see it through.

"No, no. I don't have a woman. But here, in the elevator?" He wasn't resisting her.

"It's never stopped us before," she said, stroking his dick. "Now has it?" She cut off his retort with her tongue.

Pulling her close into him, he grabbed and squeezed her breast as hard as he could. He asked her, "Ray, do you still believe in easy access?"

She placed his hand flat on her ass and said, "See for yourself."

Lifting her skirt, he ripped her pantyhose off, thrusting his finger inside her wetness. Feeling her cream, he removed his finger, and then inserted it into her mouth. "Here, taste how good you are."

As Raven sucked her nectar from his finger, Jay got a little too rough for her taste. He flipped her around, bent her over and instructed her not to bend her knees, and to make sure she kept her palms flat against the floor.

Drilling his rod deep inside her, with quick hard thrusts, he smacked her on the ass and yelled, "I told you not to bend your fucking knees!"

With a silent cry, she straightened her knees and remained still and silent until he finished raping her.

"Raven," Cassie called out, sounding as if she was off in the distance. "Raven."

"Huh?"

"Girl, where were you? I was telling you about Jay and you spaced out somewhere."

Taking a shot of Patron, Raven gathered her thoughts. "Okay, listen; this is what we're going to do."

"We? No, I don't want any part of this mess. That nigga is plum crazy. Girl, he wrapped my ass up in saran wrap."

Raven batted her eyes in disbelief. "He did what?" A slight smile crossed her face. "He wrapped you up in plastic wrap?" She fell out with laughter.

"Yes, it's funny now, but that motherfucker is crazy. I'm telling you, I ain't fucking with Jay."

"It's all good," Raven smiled. "We'll get his ass too."

"Too? We? Oh shit, I should've kept my damn mouth closed. I need another shot."

"Morgan was raped and that bastard will pay. So, I can kill two birds with one stone, no pun intended. But then again," she smiled wickedly.

"Who raped Morgan? I thought she was married."

"Yeah, well, it's a long story. And, I don't feel like going into it right now. But trust me, that guy fucked her up, and good too."

"I don't know, Raven, I—"

"You don't know? Didn't you just tell me that son-of-a-bitch wrapped your ass up in plastic wrap? And you're going to let his ass get away with that shit too?"

To her dismay, "Okay, I'm down," Cassie reluctantly agreed. "But I'm not trying to go to jail though. Not because of his raggedy ass."

"I know how to work things, trust me. You won't go to jail. Can you meet me back here at ten tonight, dressed in all black? We'll hit Jay first, and then we'll hit Thomas Whittaker."

Cassie looked confused. "Thomas Whittaker?"

"He raped Morgan."

Gasping, Cassie placed her hand over her mouth.

Chapter 30

Morgan reached over Franklin to answer her ringing cell phone. "Hello."

"Hi, Morgan. How are you feeling?"

"I'm fine, Ray. Thanks for asking."

"Um, well…"

"This is awkward. What's up?" Morgan said coolly.

"Morgan, I'm sorry. Please forgive me. Please. I can't take you not speaking to me."

"If I forgive you, then I will have to forgive Arthur, and he hasn't suffered enough," Morgan snapped.

"Mo, I think we've all suffered, too much." Sighing heavily, Raven grabbed her belly; she realized what she had to do. The thought of terminating her pregnancy riddled her with guilt and pain, but the pain she felt would not compare to the pain Morgan would feel if she ever found out. She would take care of it first thing Monday morning. "I say tonight is the night."

"For what?"

"How are you feeling, first of all? Can you move around?"

"I only have a sore ass, Ray. I'm fine."

"Good, be at my house at ten tonight, and wear black."

"You know something, I don't know what you're talking about, but I think–"

"Uh huh, don't think, just be over here. Trust me, you'll enjoy every minute of it!"

"What am I going to do with Franklin?"

"What's wrong with Arthur, he can't watch his own son?"

"I don't want Arthur doing shit for me and–"

"Franklin is his son, Mo. Besides, he did nothing wrong. It was all me."

"He had an affair with another woman, Raven. You expect me to forgive him for that?"

"Yes, I do. We all make mistakes. You made one the other night–"

"He has been trying to make it up to me."

"Mo, if you can give me a second chance, why not your husband? He does love you, and, you must admit, he is weak."

"Yeah, he's weak and I love his weak ass," she paused. "I haven't forgiven you Raven?"

Morgan's words knocked the breath from her, cutting deeper than any knife could ever cut. Tears welled in her eyes, she was at a lost for words.

"It will take some time," Morgan continued. "I'm sure, with much prayer and counseling, I will be able to forgive you. But, I will never forget. I don't know if I'll ever be able to trust you, or Arthur, to the extent as I once did. I just don't know."

Clearing a passage in her throat to speak, Raven whispered, "You don't have to forgive me, if you don't feel it's something you can do. But, for Franklin's sake, forgive Arthur. You know what it was like growing up without a father."

"Yes, no thanks to you." Although Morgan wasn't snappish, the sternest in her voice set the tone for her current demeanor.

"I know you will never let me live that down, Morgan, but I'm trying to do right. I mean, damn, I was only a child. How would I know that a beehive would kill mama and daddy?"

"You were a hellion then and you're still one!"

Clinching her teeth, Raven remained calm. "I love you. I've always loved you. I will always love you–"

"Okay, Whitney Houston!"

There was silence, before a burst of laughter eased the tension.

"Go to hell, Morgan!"

"Whatever, Sluttisha!" Morgan laughed wholeheartedly.

"Back at you, Whorina!" Raven retorted with strong laughter.

Then, deep sighs and exhales.

"I miss your laughter," Morgan said.

"I miss you, period."

Morgan ended the call with, "See you at ten."

Chapter 31

Inside his home office, Arthur studies patient files and dictates into a small hand-held recorder. Feeling her presence, he looked up at her. No smile. No smirk. Nothing. She was now feeling what he'd been feeling for weeks. Lowering his head down, focusing on the papers before him, he began writing on a writing pad. He straight carried her.

"Arthur, do you have a moment?"

"Only one moment," he said, refusing to look up at her.

"I need your full, undivided attention."

Laying the pen on the desk, he removed his reading glasses, folded them and placed them in the leather eyeglass case. "Now you want my attention." His sarcasm was thick as a rain cloud.

Morgan pointed to the chair in the corner. "May I?"

Arthur nodded.

Taking a seat, Morgan sighed heavily. "I don't know what's going to happen to us, Arthur, but I honestly can't take it anymore–"

"What are you saying? You want a divorce?"

Tilting her head to the side, she contemplated his question. Was that really what she wanted, a divorce? Lionel Richie's *Hello* was playing through the tiny radio behind Arthur's desk.

"I'm not sure what else I can do, Morgan. I mean, I've groveled, I've begged, I've done everything except kill myself. I just don't know," he paused, and looked at her. "You kept your word."

"What do you mean?"

Clasping his hands together, intertwining his fingers, he laid his head back against the high back leather executive chair and closed his eyes. "You wanted me to hurt as much as I had hurt you. Well, it does hurt, Mo. The idea of you being with another man hurts me deeply. But, what practically killed me was seeing you on a *date* with another man. I can't say that I blame you. I suppose you feel as though you must move on with your life, and if that were the case, then a divorce would be necessary. But, I didn't think you'd move on so fast."

Staring wordlessly at Arthur, as tears flowed over her full cheeks, Morgan, with all she had within her, she mustered the words, "He raped me."

Arthur's brows pulled into an affronted frown. His jaws clenched, his eyes slightly narrowed, he spoke softly and with concern. "I will kill the son-of-a-bitch!"

Wiping away her sorrow with the back of her hand, Morgan sniffed a couple of times before speaking. "He will be taken care of." She thought about Raven and knew she had something up her sleeve, as did she.

"Are you all right?"

She nodded.

Standing, he walked over to her and knelt down before her. "Are you sure you're okay?"

"I'm fine, Arthur. Raven took me to the hospital and–"

"Raven?"

Again, she nodded. "I didn't know who else to call."

"You could've called me."

Shaking her head, she smiled and then cupped his face in her hand. "I couldn't have called you, baby. I couldn't have faced you for anything in the world after that night. It took all I had to face you now."

He kissed the palm of her hand and caressed her knee. "So, you and Raven...you two are back on speaking terms?"

"I'm not without fault, Arthur."

"I love you so–"

She pressed her thin finger against his lips. "Hush. I know you love me. We'll get through this. I know we will." She leaned in and kissed his lips. It was the softest kiss he'd ever felt in his life. "I love you too."

"Well," she sighed, "I need to get ready."

"Where are you going?"

"To meet with Raven. Will you watch Franklin?"

He nodded and smiled. "Yeah. I can do that."

Chapter 32

Patron was the centerpiece for the dining room table as the plan was mapped out and placed into action.

"Are we ready to do this, my sistahs?"

"Raven, I don't know–"

"Cassie, it will be okay." Morgan looked toward Raven. "I'm ready!"

"What if we get caught?" Cassie inquired, as small beads of perspiration begin to form around the edges of her hairline.

"We won't get caught," Raven said. "You're in the company of two pros when it comes to this shit," she laughed. Checking the time on her watch, Raven looked at Morgan, who was sitting to her right, the perfect place for her right hand. "Are you ready to make that call?"

Morgan nodded.

"Okay, take deep breaths," Cassie said.

"I'm cool. Give me the phone."

"Okay, here," said Raven, passing her cell phone to Morgan. "Block the call first—*67."

"Got it!" Morgan dialed the number and quietly listened to three rings before the call was picked up. "Hi, Thomas, it's

Morgan. How are you? That's good. I wanted to call and thank you for such a good time, the other night. Uh huh. Really? Okay, well, you and I must hook up again, sometime soon. Sounds good to you? Okay, I'll be in touch. Take it easy. Bye."

"You talked too much," Raven said, after Morgan ended the call.

"I did what I was supposed to do. I called to make sure his ass was home and he is."

"Let's roll out."

Dressed in black, the three ninjas headed out the door.

"This is kind of exciting," Cassie giggled.

"We should have gotten a rental car," Morgan said, as Raven parked two houses down from Thomas Whittaker's townhouse.

"Rental car or my car, my name will be attached. So, it doesn't matter. Besides, he won't get the chance to see what we're driving."

"I'm scared y'all," Cassie whimpered.

"Trust me," Raven said, "Your adrenaline will start pumping the minute you step foot in dude's place. Ready?"

With a black satchel, they climbed out of the car and, like predators in the night, headed toward Whittaker's front door. They rung the doorbell and slipped wool caps over their faces, holes exposing their eyes, nose and lips. When the door opened, they bombarded Whittaker and forced him back inside the house.

"What the fuck is going on?"

Pinning him against the wall, the feminine voice asked, "Are you Thomas Whittaker?"

He was silent.

"Answer me, motherfucker!"

"Yeah...yes, I am."

Quickly, they led him to the sofa and tossed him face down. Then, Cassie sat on his back, holding him down.

"What are you going to do? Please don't hurt me, please!"

With her fist, Morgan punched him in the back of the head. "Shut the fuck up, bitch!"

Raven tied his wrists and legs together with string she pulled from the black satchel. "Sit him up," she ordered.

Moving close to Raven, Morgan whispered, "Let me fuck his ass up, real quick."

"Do you, baby girl."

Stepping in close to him, Morgan closed her hand into a fist. She drew back her arm and, within a blink of an eye, she plowed her fist, fast forward toward his face, landing on his nose. Blood sprayed from his broken nose. Again, she drew her arm back and released another powerful blow to his face. After the fifth blow to his face, Whittaker was unrecognizable.

"That's enough, girl," Cassie laughed, looking down at Whittaker. "You got knocked the fuck out!"

Pulling a strap-on dildo from the satchel, Raven held it up.

"What's that?" Morgan asked.

"Karma. What goes around comes around. Time for old boy to get fucked in his ass."

Morgan stood erect. "Oh, I can't do that...I mean—"

"Fine. I'll do it. Take off his pants and turn him over."

Whittaker was out cold, thanks to Sugar Ray Morgan.

Morgan and Cassie turned him over and pulled his pants down around his ankles, while Raven took off her pants.

"Wait, why are you taking off your pants?" asked Cassie.

"Girl, there's a clit tickler inside the strap. I might as well get mine while he's gettin' his."

Straddling Whittaker's behind, Raven inched her fingers between his cheeks, spreading them far apart, stretching open his asshole. "A pretty asshole," she chuckled.

"Girl, will you just do it and let's get the fuck out of here," Morgan said.

No grease. No KY-Jelly. No saliva. Raven aimed the head of the rubber dildo at his opening and rammed it deep inside, bringing Whittaker out of his coma.

As he yelled to the top of his lungs, almost as if someone had cut his dick off, Raven yelled, "Put something in his mouth, quick!"

Cassie pulled his sock off his foot and shoved it inside his mouth.

Reaching inside the satchel, Morgan pulled out the saran wrap, tore off a long piece and wrapped it around his face, three times.

"Damn, this shit is turning me on. I'm about to come. Y'all should try this shit, it feels good!"

"Come already so we can go!" said Morgan.

Whittaker began choking on his cries, unable to breathe.

"He can't breathe," said Cassie.

"So? Fuck him," said Morgan, as she grabbed Raven by the arm. "Let's go!"

Pulling the dildo from Whittaker's blood-ridden rectum, she wiped off the dildo on his sofa, stuffed it inside the bag and slipped on her pants.

With her gloved hand, Morgan frantically wiped down all surfaces, as Cassie darted into the kitchen. Under the sink, she found a bottle of bleach. Returning to the living room, she tore the top off the bottle and poured it all over Whittaker and the sofa.

Whittaker painfully cried when the bleach hit the raw meat around the opening of his rectum.

"What are you doing that for?" Raven asked.

"You took your pants off. You fucked him on the sofa."

"So?"

"Girl, do you watch CSI: New York?" She huffed in annoyance. "Pieces of your skin are probably in the sofa, on his ass, everything."

"Damn, good looking out," Morgan said, running into the kitchen and returning with a bottle of ammonia. She poured the contents of the bottle over the sofa and on Whittaker. "There," she said, throwing the bottle at the back of his head, leaving him to inhale a deadly, toxic gas from the ammonia, bleach mixture. "That should do it. Let's roll!"

Chapter 33

In the parking lot of Park Southern Apartments, Cassie, Raven and Morgan went over the game plan. With Jay, they had to make sure they carried it out to a tee.

Raven handed Cassie the phone. "Call him, and *67 the call."

Doing as instructed, Cassie was scared as shit. At Whittaker's, she was cool, because she didn't know him. But she knew Jay, and new him well. She just fucked him a few days ago.

"Hey, Jay, it's Cassie. I haven't heard anything from you about the plan for Raven. Did you decide against it? Oh, you didn't? Okay, well you will let me know, right? I'm ready to get in that bitch's ass! Huh? Change of mind. Oh, yeah, well…I can't stop thinking about Marcy. You know? Okay, call me later. Bye."

"You talk too damn much too," Raven snapped.

Climbing the stairs to apartment 304, Raven tapped on the door.

"Who is it?" Jay yelled from inside the apartment.

"It's me," Cassie said.

"I just got off the phone with you," he said, opening the door.

They pushed their way inside his apartment, shoving him and pushing him into the kitchen.

"What kinda shit is this? Who the fuck is you bitch's?"

Raven removed her cap and stared him square in the eyes. "It's me, you punk ass mother fucker!" Before he could speak, her fist landed in his mouth, knocking his head back against the cabinet.

Jay wasn't being taken down without a fight. He began to swing, a punch landing on Raven's cheek. She fell backward. Eyeing the frying pan on the stove, Morgan grabbed it and bashed Jay in the back of the head, fried chicken greased splattered everywhere. Jay fell to the floor.

"Are you okay?" Morgan asked Raven, helping her up off the floor.

"Yeah, I'm fine. Let's wrap this bastard up."

Within minutes, Jay was wrapped from head to toe in saran wrap, gasping for air.

Ain't karma a bitch?

"Okay, clean up, y'all," Morgan said.

As Jay wiggled around on the kitchen floor like a fish out of water, gasping and choking for air, taking his last breaths, Morgan doused the walls of the kitchen with ammonia and bleach. "I got this from Cassie," she smiled, wondering what would kill him first; the plastic wrap, or toxic fumes.

"Do we have anymore unfinished business, ladies?"
They all looked at each other and fell out with laughter.

Other Xpress Yourself Publishing Titles
P.O. Box 1615, Upper Marlboro, Maryland 20773, Attn: Book Sales

QTY	TITLE/AUTHOR	ISBN-13	PRICE
	Anything Goes/Jessica Tilles	978-0-972990-0-8	$15.00
	In My Sisters' Corner/Jessica Tilles	978-0-9722990-1-5	$15.00
	Apple Tree/Jessica Tilles	978-0-9722990-2-2	$15.00
	Sweet Revenge/Jessica Tilles	978-0-9722990-3-9	$15.00
	Fatal Desire/Jessica Tilles	978-09722990-5-3	$15.00
	One Love/Bill Holmes	978-0-9722990-4-6	$15.00
	Dangerously/Makenzi	978-0-9722990-7-7	$15.00
	That's How I Like It/Makenzi	978-0-9722990-8-4	$15.00
	Love Changes/Michael J. Burt	978-0-9722990-6-0	$10.95
	For Every Love There Is A Reason/ Kenda Bell	978-0-9722990-9-1	$16.95
	Unfinished Business/Jessica Tilles	978-0-9792500-0-2	$15.00
	Confessions of a Sex Therapist/Nyah Storm	978-09792500-2-6	$15.00
	How Do I Go On?/Lonnie Spry	978-09792500-3-3	$15.00
	Tonight I Give In/Mia A. Moore (June 2007)	978-09792500-7-1	$15.00
	Let the Necessary Occur/Gayle Jackson Sloan (Fall 2007)	978-09792500-5-7	$15.00
	A Life Beyond Limits: Overcoming Private Pain/Nataki Suggs (June 2007)	978-09792500-9-5	$10.95
	How Men Cheat/Sherman Barrett (Available June 2007)	978-09792500-8-8	$15.00
	Straight From My Heart/Bill Holmes (June 2007)	978-09792500-6-4	$10.95
	A Whisper to a Scream/Elissa Gabrielle (Fall 2007)	978-09792500-1-9	$15.00
	Erogenous Zone: A Sexual Voyage An Anthology (August 2007)	978-09792500-4-0	$15.00

www.xpressyourselfpublishing.org

I am enclosing $____ (plus $3.50 shipping for 1st book, $1.00 for each additional book). No cash or C.O.D.s please. Send check, money order, certified check or credit card payment to:

Xpress Yourself Publishing
P.O. Box 1615
Upper Marlboro, MD 20773
Attn: Book Sales.

Please allow 2 to 4 weeks for delivery. Fax credit card orders to (202) 478-3447 for same day processing.

Name _____

Address _____

City _____ State _____ Zip Code _____

For credit card payments, please complete the following:

_____ American Express _____ MasterCard _____ Visa

Card Holder Name: _____

Account #: _____Exp. Date: _____

Total amount to be charged: $_____

Authorized Signature: _____
Date: _____
Note: Credit Cards are the preferred form of payment.

LaVergne, TN USA
17 September 2010
197457LV00002B/61/A